I0452899

CRAVING:
A TERRAMATES NOVEL

LISA LACE

CRAVING
Copyright © 2016 Toppings Publishing.
All rights reserved.

Disclaimer

This book is licensed for your personal enjoyment only.

Copyright Notes

No part of this publication may be used or reproduced in any form or by any means, including printing, photocopying, or otherwise, without written permission from the author, except in the case of brief quotations embodied in critical articles or review.

If you would like to use material from the book (other than just simply for reviewing the book), prior permission must be obtained by contacting the author at lisa@lisalace.com.

CONTENTS

CHAPTER 1

Kai Imwaden wondered if someone was going to die today.

He poked his head over the edge of an arena box in the stadium hosting today's wedding battle. Similar seating was reserved for invited nobles and spread out in a wide semi-circle at a tier in the middle portion of the arena. Bodies filled every seat. The main event featured the wedding of his uncle, Prince Hanton of the Anquera, and the princess of a recently conquered world, one the Anquesh considered an honored enemy. Their battlefield prowess had earned them a special status among the Anquesh's acquisitions.

The fact that Shinalor was rich in ores and minerals the Anquesh needed for other war efforts was a nice bonus.

The rules of the fight were simple. If the male defeated the female in combat, she was his, and the rest of the marriage ceremony began immediately. If the woman prevailed, or the man fled the arena, the marriage was considered void, and any treaties based on the union were invalid.

A hot midday breeze whipped up the sides of a tent in the middle of the arena, revealing a pensive warrior pacing around the interior of his symbolic home. Hanton knew the importance of successfully defeating his bride in combat, but rumors around the palace suggested the man was besotted with the exotic princess from Shinalor, and might be wary of hurting her. Kai had spotted the princess in the gym yesterday, furiously working with a sparring partner. This bride wasn't going to submit without a fight. Her face showed pride, and the princess would do anything to win her freedom.

He didn't blame her. Kai possessed no desire to get married. When he entered the military, he decided marriage wasn't part of his immediate future. Constant rotations to new posts would make it impossible for him to attend to his husbandly duties. He could find a bride to propagate his line when he was older and retired from the service.

Kai shifted uncomfortably, trying to adjust his uniform. Even though he was in the shade of a tented stadium box, the midday sun reflected lots of heat onto his outfit. His breastplate consisted of a lightweight, sturdy metal from one of the Empire's conquests. It was best suited to deflect the blasts from energy weapons. The armor came with a matching sword that was more than a costume piece. Its edge was permanently sharp and could easily sever the head from an opponent.

He was proud to wear the uniform of a highly-ranked military officer, no matter how hot it was.

In the morning, his valet had put out the new clothing without commenting. Kai hoped it meant he was getting to command a spaceship. He felt like he deserved that honor, but promotions in the military were slow because of his father.

It was difficult being the stepson of the Emperor and the son of an unpopular wife. The Emperor was careful to avoid rumors of favoritism and never showed any influence on Kai's career. In fact, some commanders delighted in abusing Kai and intimidating him. The struggles only drove Kai to excellence. He had recently earned him a post as the youngest instructor in the Anquera Battle Academy.

His mother glided to his side. She usually appeared radiant, and today the Crown Princess Andeleth wore an embroidered silk gown. The blue dress glowed faintly in graduated hues from the hem to the bodice.

He leaned forward and kissed her cheek. "You're looking well."

She hummed as she took a center seat. "Come here. Sit next to me."

"It's too hot," Kai said with a small groan.

"You're too old to complain about things you cannot change."

"I've heard rumors of other planets where they can cool the air with machines," Kai said.

"Have you been listening to reports about our enemy again?" sniffed the princess. "You shouldn't envy or admire the humans. Their technology comes at a price. They have polluted their planet. Only a fraction of their land is arable. It's better to focus research on ways to defeat your enemy, like we do."

"But they manage to feed billions of people on that portion. We'd be fortunate to do half as well."

"Make sure you don't let your stepfather hear you say those things. Every resource in our empire goes to fighting Earth. He is upset about the situation."

"They are a formidable foe," Kai agreed. "I read the intelligence reports, mother, and learned from those studies. The humans match up well with us. They're lacking in physical strength, but they make up for it with superior tactics and technology. I've reviewed their strategic maneuvers. They are adaptive and responsive. They make plans within plans."

"Your teaching at the Academy has drawn a lot of praise."

"Has it?" said Kai slyly. "How? No one's said anything to me."

"It's not for me to say, my son. Your stepfather wants to make the announcement."

"At his brother's marriage ceremony?"

His mother shrugged. "A successful marriage and a new appointment are both good for the morale of the nation. There's no need to hide our successes from the people and every reason to share them."

"Only if Hanton wins the fair Tatianna." Kai smiled wickedly. "Did you know the bookies give her a forty percent chance of winning her way out of the marriage?"

Andeleth made a small derisive noise for Kai's benefit. "If she puts up a good fight, it only adds to our house's honor."

Kai cocked an eyebrow. "If you believe that superstition, why did you submit to the Emperor without a fight on your wedding day?" When others had asked her the same question, the princess always replied with a mysterious smile. Today's response was different.

"I knew he was my sindare, and he knew I was his. We didn't need to battle each other at all."

The admission was surprising to Kai. It confirmed the rumors titillating the court at the time - people said that Emperor Kanton and Andeleth did more than hold hands before the wedding. There were only two ways to confirm if a prospective mate was also a fated love: either battle or the bedroom. Most Anquesh women would rather submit to the pressure of the first than the scandal of the second.

Apparently his mother was an exception.

"I knew the moment he took my hand during our introduction." Her eyes twinkled. "Of course, being a male, it took a little more for your stepfather to recognize the evidence in front of his eyes."

"Mother, I'm shocked at your wanton ways," Kai said with a chuckle.

The loud steps of the Emperor's retinue preceded the man himself. They spread out in chairs lined up behind the royal family's seats. As usual, the Emperor looked grim-faced until he saw his sindare. The sight made him break out into a bright smile.

"Light of my life," he said, taking her hand. "The morning dragged until now."

Andeleth took his hand. If they were alone, she might have given the Emperor an intimate greeting, but in public, it was inappropriate to do more than squeeze his hand lightly.

"My lord." Andeleth gave a smile of her own.

Kanton looked around. "Where is my son?"

"Right here, father." Crown Prince Warrel entered with his retainers, taking up the remaining chairs in the box.

Warrel wore a dress uniform without battle accouterments. As the heir to the throne, he was forbidden to serve in the military. Even though Warrel needed to be ready in case the Emperor died unexpectedly, the inability to serve was a blow to the psyche of any Anquesh male. It was important to fight and win honors in battle.

Kai understood Warrel's dilemma and tried to look deferential to his stepbrother. But Warrel made things difficult with jibes and insults when he thought no one was looking.

The Prince's eyes widened when he saw Kai's new dress uniform. They narrowed again when he realized Kai was about to receive another military honor. He looked away, distinctly unhappy.

"Son," said Kanton sharply, "I'm certain the Emperor is supposed to enter last."

Ouch, thought Kai. A public reprimand must have hurt the Prince's pride.

"Yes, honored father," said Warrel with a small bow. "Please forgive my breach of protocol."

"Well, let's not think about it too much. I've had you working hard scheduling troop deployments. You were thinking about matters of state, no doubt. Now that Kai's finished his assignment at the Academy, he can assist with that task."

Kai felt Warrel's cold gaze sweep his body. He didn't want Kai's help.

"Of course." The voice sounded even and controlled. But a hateful glance at Kai revealed the Prince's feelings for his stepbrother. Kai held back a sigh.

Things would never change with Warrel.

CHAPTER 2

After a long day at work, all Jennifer Carden wanted to do was lie down on her couch and think about nothing. She reached for the remote and turned on the TV, which displayed a news channel.

That was a mistake.

All the news focused on the war with the Anquesh. Today an enterprising paparazzo had managed to get a clear shot of an Anquesh warrior. Jenn wondered if the photographer got a bonus for making the alien soldier look as frightening as possible.

The Anquesh in the video was huge, perhaps seven feet tall with bulging muscles. With his dark hair twirled in dreadlocks, a scowling face, arms covered in tattoos and fearsome armor, he looked like a killing machine.

The alien soldier leered at the screen, then raised his hand and batted away the camera, making the picture go dark. Jenn heard metal clattering on the floor. The cameraman screamed, begging for his life. Even in a war movie, she'd never seen or heard anything that gruesome.

Earth first encountered the Anquesh during a deep space expedition. No one knew what had happened during that first contact incident, but in the end, the Earth had found a new enemy alien race that wanted to conquer the planet.

Jenn shivered. She couldn't imagine getting so close to an Anquesh warrior that they could touch her.

Besides their intimidating physical experience, another thing contributing to her fear was that the Anquesh killed her father. He was an infantry soldier fighting on the front lines of a planet so far away from Earth that Jenn would be an old woman if he ever came back home. Her mother died of a heart attack soon after they received the news of his death.

At the time, faster-than-light travel was a one-way trip. Since her father's service, scientists had discovered a way to bend the law of relativity which let flights return to Earth faster.

Her phone rang, showing a video of her friend Nayla tapping restlessly on the phone. Jenn chuckled. Nayla never liked to wait for anything.

"Hey, girl," said Jenn.

"Damn. What were you doing? Kissing your boyfriend's ass again?"

Jenn laughed. "Anton's not here right now."

"Good. Let's go to Nardones for pizza."

"Nope."

"What? Tai Chi class again?"

Jenn had increased her Tai Chi participation. One of the responsibilities of her stressful job was dealing with battered and severely injured soldiers. She tried to find relief for herself in the ancient exercise.

"I wish. I can't afford it."

"Didn't you just get a raise?"

Jenn sighed. "Yes, but it pushed me into the next tax bracket. I'm not making as much as you might expect." The problem wasn't only taxes. The trust fund created from her mother's insurance money placed her in a high tax bracket anyway, but Nayla didn't know that. All she knew was that her best friend had a great paying job.

"That sucks. People aren't going to stand for that much longer."

"What are we going to do? We all need to pay our share for the war effort."

"Yup, just like we are supposed to support our local businesses. Let's support Nardones!"

The thought of pizza made Jenn's mouth water. She hadn't eaten out for a few months. Anton never seemed to have any credits, and ever since her roommate left to get married, money had been tight. Sure, the trust fund existed in an emergency, but she didn't like to use it. She associated the fund with feelings of loss and her mother's death. Jenn couldn't bear to spend a cent of that chunk of cash.

"You know what would help me support our merchants? If you moved in with me and helped with the rent, we could eat out all the time."

In the beginning, the war was good for the Earth's economy, in particular for any company supplying the military. But as the fighting drew out, Earth's resources diminished and military budgets increased. Taxes all over the world were at an all-time high. Businesses that weren't part of the war effort had two problems: competing with the government for the diminishing discretionary cash of the people, and keeping prices down so people could buy goods and services. The government encouraged people to spend money as much as possible. The world banks said everyone would get richer.

Nayla wrinkled her nose. "No thanks. When you ditch Anton, then we'll talk about it."

"You could come over here, at least. I have chili leftovers from last night."

"No, I had my heart set on pizza tonight." She paused thoughtfully. "Besides, your boy is due to come home soon, isn't he?"

Jenn shrugged. "I never know. He works irregular hours."

"Please, girl. The one thing we can count on is Anton showing up for a free meal. He'll be there."

As if Nayla were psychic, the lock turned in Jenn's door.

"Speak of the devil. Your predictions are eerily accurate. If we could package that ability and sell it to the military, our money troubles would be over."

LISA LACE

Nayla scoffed. "Our money troubles? Sweetie, if I scored a military contract, I wouldn't be sharing it with you."

Although her friend pretended to be joking, Jenn knew she was telling the truth. Nayla had a part-time job. She'd been up against the wall trying to meet expenses and still lived with her grandmother. Nayla had only asked Jenn out because she knew that as soft-hearted as Jenn was, she would end up paying the bill.

Jenn didn't mind. Nayla had been her best friend ever since they found themselves in the same foster home. Nayla always had Jenn's back.

At least Jenn had a full-time job. Many employers had cut expenses to the bone, so jobs were scarce. Fortunately for Jenn, in a war economy, one thing was always in demand: medical services. Jenn was a licensed physical therapist. She spent her days helping wounded soldiers train their bodies how to move again. For some of them, it was a long, hard struggle. From what Jenn saw working with her patients, she knew the Anquesh were murdering bastards.

Anton walked in. A scarf and fedora covered his handsome face to protect against the cold. He took the hat and scarf off, as well as his wool coat, and put them on a side chair next to the couch. Jenn smiled when she saw him.

"I've got to go. Tell you what. Let's catch a movie tomorrow night instead. There's a special at the Metro and we can get free popcorn."

16

"You've got a date."

Anton bent over and gave her a kiss on the cheek.

"Was that Nayla?" he asked, cocking an eyebrow. Anton and Nayla had never gotten along. "Why are you making plans for a Friday night? I thought that was our special time together."

"Is that chintzy little kiss all you have for me?" she pouted.

"It is until you have an answer."

Jenn scoffed. "I don't have any answers. It's not like you're my husband or anything."

He sighed heavily. "Not this again. If I've told you once, I've told you a hundred times. I need to get my finances in order before I get married to anyone."

"It doesn't seem like you ever will," she muttered. Her happiness at seeing Anton vanished under the cloud of their old argument.

"I won't be as long if you keep pressuring me," he snapped. The disapproving expression on Anton's face and something about the way he stood over her caused a wave of anger to wash over Jenn. She suddenly stood up from the couch.

"I don't think two years is pressuring you." Jenn's tone of voice was frosty.

"I just need a little time, Jenn." Panic was showing on his face now, and she liked that. How long did she need to keep being the nice girl? How long did she need to keep making meals and watch movies on the television because he didn't have money to take them out? How long did she have to keep dishing out money because he 'forgot' to go the bank?

"You know what? I think I've had enough. It's better to be alone than having you string me along."

"Jenn, I never did that to you. We can figure this out. Let's not mess up a good thing." He was pleading now, but the years of frustration and disappointment built up in her heart were finally erupting. Jenn held up her hands.

"You know what? I'm done. Give me your key and get out of here."

"Don't do this. I'm sorry. You're right. I've put things off, but only because I had something special planned."

Jenn's eyes narrowed. "That sounds convenient. What's your big surprise?"

"I wanted to present something more elaborate, but I guess I don't have a lot of time." He went to his coat and took out a small box and handed it to her.

Jenn's heart leaped, but she didn't want to be disappointed. She cautiously opened the box to discover a sparkling engagement ring. She stared it without speaking.

"Do you like it?" he asked.

She swallowed hard and felt ashamed. "But you said you wanted to wait."

"I was stalling, but I guess I was doing it in the worst possible way. Let me make it up to you. This weekend we'll go to Vegas and get married. Just you, me and Elvis. We'll do the whole deal. Vows, cake, dinner at the fanciest restaurant we can go to without reservations, and a honeymoon suite in one of the hotels. What do you think?"

"This weekend?" Her voice rose. Jenn couldn't believe what was happening. She had waited her entire life to get married, and suddenly it was going to happen.

"Of course, babe. That's why I didn't want you to go out with Nayla tomorrow night. I was going to take you for a drive and go straight to Vegas."

"You were going to surprise me?" Random gestures were uncharacteristic of Anton, but at the moment, she was so surprised and happy that she didn't want to overthink her good fortune.

Anton lifted her chin up so he could look Jenn in the eyes. "It won't be the best wedding in the world, but we'll be married. What do you say?"

Jenn bounced on her toes and wrapped her arms around Anton's neck. "Yes!"

CHAPTER 3

The voice of Kai's tactical officer, Jod, screamed out of his headset. "Ten more ships have joined the alien fleet."

"Only ten," growled Kai. "It might as well be fifty. What does our firepower look like?"

"No ships have any long-range cannons remaining. The bastards targeted each one after their first volleys. Only short-range lasers are left."

The Anquesh long-range pulse cannons were effective mechanisms for destruction. It was why the Earth spaceships prioritized those weapons as a target.

Kai shook his head. He couldn't possible engage the enemy with short-range weapons, not with ten fresh enemy ships waiting to destroy them.

On the monitor, both the new and old enemy ships sat silently, mocking them with their presence.

"I have our shields at full strength again, but our long-range cannon needs further repairs."

"Noted, chief." Kai needed to think, and the constant interruptions from his crew were distracting.

Kai had been incredibly happy a few months ago when the Emperor gave him command of a sector flagship, a responsibility that usually went to a much older warrior. His crew felt pleased by association. They were proud to follow a member of the royal family. Who was Kai to remind them that officially he was still a commoner?

It didn't matter to them, anyway. When the Emperor ordered his stepson to the front lines of the war, it showed his confidence in the Anquera war effort. The Emperor wouldn't intentionally send Kai to his death. The move was politically savvy and rewarded Kai for service to the empire.

Kai felt humiliated that he was failing.

The Earth ships appeared to use signal deflection technology to mask their presence. But it only worked if the ships maintained their position. Had they waited for days or weeks until a hapless Anquesh battle group crossed their path? Kai's squad was on a standard border patrol when the Earth ships struck them in a move that surprised all his officers and crew.

One minute empty space stretched in front of them. In the next, a barrage of laser fire blasted into the unsuspecting Anquesh battleships.

Five ships of the line were disabled in that skirmish and were currently dealing with failing systems. The ships that remained battle-worthy were scrambling to complete repairs before they encountered the enemy again.

They had run out of time.

Kai looked at the battlefield map projected on the holoscreen in the center of the command deck. Ten more enemy ships had appeared. But where did they come from?

Did Earth have a new cloaking technology? A faster, better engine? Anything was possible, but Anquera had heard no rumors of surprises from Earth.

His ships positioned themselves in a semi-circle flanking his vessel, the Ruvien, but half of them were too damaged to fight. His hands passed over different places on the map, magnifying the view of the enemy fleet and bringing various locations into focus.

The Earth ships remained in their original position. It was a clear stretch of space. There were no planets, asteroids or nebulas to hide reinforcements. Where did they get ten additional ships?

Humans fought differently than the Anquesh, and Kai found it difficult to put himself in their shoes. Most Anquesh commanders would rush all their ships into battle immediately, but the Earth fleet wasn't moving. They must be damaged.

He continued to study the map as his officers reported on each ship in the sector group. Kai heard defeat in the voices of his officers. The arrival of the new Earth ships didn't only provide reinforcements. Their sudden appearance was meant to demoralize their enemy. And it was working.

But there was no way they could be there.

An enemy round of laser fire jolted the Ruvien. It was a relatively weak blast, but Kai fell against the base of the holoscreen rising from the deck. His hand passed harmlessly through the holoscreen.

"Jod, order our functional ships to follow us. Tell the damaged ships to hold back. They only have one long-range weapon and its charge must be weak. Otherwise, they would have continued attacking all our ships. We're going to take this opportunity to strike at close range. I don't think the extra ten ships exist."

"We have definite signatures on all the engines."

"Then they're very clever holographic projections, or something designed to trick our sensors. They can't be there, so they aren't."

"Yes, sir!" Jod said reluctantly. Kai was sure the man questioned his sanity, but he was confident the soldier would carry out his orders. Kai hoped that the rest of his crew would follow the chain of command, despite his failures of the past few hours.

He listened to the orders and various reports of the Ruvien's repair status. They put the shields at maximum strength by taking power from the life support systems. A third of the decks were evacuated and sealed.

Many crew members were injured, but the medical bay operated under triage protocols and only accepted people with life-threatening injuries. Anyone with medical training was being pulled from their regular duties so they could attend the wounded.

Time slowed down as Kai watched his embattled sector group advance on the Earth ships. It was a slow dance that would end in death. If the Anquesh emerged victoriously, it would be by the will of the gods.

The battle board flashed as they arrived at the engagement point. It was far point from the enemy ships, but their weapons could hit their targets. Kai didn't want to wait.

"Fire!" His voice rumbled through the communications system of his ship. Blue laser blasts hit the lead ship, causing explosions and making the Earth vessel start to list.

A cheer went up around the bridge, but Kai knew better than to join in. He saw the forward ship recover quickly when the Ruvien moved in for the kill. The enemy ship fired for the first time, attacking the Ruvien. The Anquesh vessel groaned, and a new round of electrical fires ignited on the bridge.

An explosion tossed Kai in the air, and he landed awkwardly on the deck. He smelled the chemical scent of bulkheads melting. Kai lifted himself up from the deck to survey the damage. The bridge crew was already moving to put out the fires, but the smoke made it difficult for everyone to breathe. Wincing, Kai dragged himself to the command chair and dropped heavily into it.

"Commander, we're receiving an incoming communication from the enemy ship."

"Put it on screen," said Kai. It didn't matter what the humans wanted to say. The conversation would allow his crew to recover for a few minutes.

When the image of the human flashed in front of him, Kai was surprised at the sight of the alien. He could never tell the ages of humans. Most were the size of a large child. This one's hair was white and black, with more light than dark in it. Blood trickled from his forehead.

"This is Commodore Jeff Bretland. I respectfully ask for a conference with the commander of your battle group." He spoke in reasonably good Anquesh, which impressed Kai.

"That's me," said Kai, replying in Standard. "Commander Kai Imwaden."

"So it's true. They sent a member of the royal family."

"I am commander of the battle group, and that's all you need to know."

"There's no need to be an ass."

Bretland spat out a word in English. Kai's communications officer spoke the translation in his ear piece. "It's a pejorative in their language, sir."

"I know what it is," muttered Kai.

"I came here specifically to speak with you. All of our other attempts at communication have failed. We hoped that by communicating directly with a member of the royal family, someone will hear our proposal."

"You are speaking many words but not saying anything, Commodore."

"You're right. I'll get to the point. I would say we've fought this battle to a draw. It's what we intended."

"You did?" Kai did not believe Bretland was telling the truth.

"Yes. We know your culture values strong warriors. If we came to you with our offer without being willing to fight, you would classify us as weaklings. We'll never back down from a fight, but we don't have the resources for a perpetual war. Commander Imwaden, we believe Anquera is in a similar situation. If we continue fighting each other, we think it plays right into the hands of one of your allies. They're pretending to be your friend, but secretly they want to see you exhausted and unprepared to fight on a second front when they decide to attack."

"Who is it?" growled Kai. "Say the name of the betrayers." A cold shiver ran through his body when he realized the humans had access to intelligence that should be classified. How did they know his name?

"I will happily share information with Anquera if you accept our peace proposal. Commander, any race that wants to conquer you won't stop there. They'll go after Earth as well. It only makes sense for us to cease hostilities and work together to prevent our mutual destruction."

The bridge crew stared at Commodore Bretland. Some began to talk among themselves. Others gripped their workstations tightly until their knuckles got white. Kai pursed his lips.

"I do not know how the Emperor will feel about the notion of peace. I'm not his emissary. But I am willing to speak with him."

The human looked relieved.

"You'll have to come with me. Wait for my communication."

Kai signaled his communications officer to stop the data stream. When the video stopped transmitting, Kai's crew turned to him blankly.

"Get on with your duties! You heard everything. We're going home, and we're taking the Earth spaceships with us."

Kai sank into his chair. The pain in his shoulder started to spread up his neck and sparked a headache. But a small injury was better than a large one, and life was preferable to death. He would take these Earth soldiers home and let someone else deal with their strange proposal.

CHAPTER 4

"Damn it!" Jenn fumbled the key in her lock. As she shifted her weight and tried to force the doorknob, her grocery bag ripped open, spilling the contents onto the floor. Sighing, she bent over to pick them up. Her hair fell from behind her ears to the front of her face. When she swept it back, she saw two pairs of legs in front of her. She stood quickly, examining the two men who had appeared at the top of the stairs.

The first wore an expensive-looking black wool coat but looked a little rough. His predatory gaze swept over her slowly, like he wanted to eat her. Jenn immediately felt uncomfortable. The second man, who stood behind the first, didn't have the same sense of fashion as his friend. He had a hardness in his eyes that made Jenn shiver.

"Can I help you?" she asked, working hard to keep her voice as steady as possible.

"I'm looking for Anton Meliknec. Someone said he spends time here."

Spends time here? Jenn thought that was a strange way to talk about the place where Anton lived with his wife.

"I suppose he does, but he's not right now."

"Anton's never around when you need him. Do me a favor. Tell him Jimmy is looking for his money, and he don't have much time to come up with it."

A million questions flew through her mind, but she knew better than to voice her concerns. Who was Jimmy? And why did Anton owe him money? It was true that things were going badly in Anton's construction business. The state hadn't paid a dime yet for his road construction project. Even if these people were suppliers looking for their money, that didn't give them the right to come here and bother her. Jenn had enough financial problems just paying the apartment bills. She hoped these men would leave her alone.

"Like I said, he's not here. I'd appreciate it if you didn't come back."

The man snorted. "Did you hear that, Guido? She doesn't want us to come back."

Jennifer had never known a nice man named Guido. He grinned in a manner that reminded Jenn of a gargoyle on a church roof.

"We won't have to return if Anton comes up with the money, boss." Guido's tone sounded snarky, and Jenn realized she couldn't stop them from returning if she tried. As the wool coat man descended the stairs, he looked back at Jenn with anger in his eyes.

"Do yourself a favor. Tell Anton he needs to pay up, and fast."

What the fuck? thought Jenn in alarm. *What the hell is going on here?*

The encounter had shaken her so much that she could barely get her key in the door again. When she finally managed to open her apartment, she gracelessly stumbled into it. Jenn immediately shut her door and turned the deadbolt. After she placed the groceries on the kitchen table, she tried to call Anton, but he didn't answer his phone.

Jenn switched on the television. Hearing other voices made her feel like she wasn't alone, even if they were noises coming out of an electronic box. She poured a glass of wine for herself and pulled out a cutting board to chop vegetables as a newscast played in the background.

The United Earth Alliance battle group headed by Commodore Jeff Bretland is reported missing in action. Information is sparse on this newest development in the war with the Anquesh Empire, and United Earth Alliance Military have no comment on the matter. There are ten battlecruiser-class ships in Commodore Bretland's group.

Commodore Bretland is a highly decorated veteran of the Anquesh War, earning his first field commission at the battle of Harmony Gate. He achieved the rank of Commodore and took charge of Panther Battlegroup in September.

Jenn tuned out the television. Her thoughts drifted back to the unpleasant encounter with the men outside her door. She picked up her phone and texted Anton.

You need to come home.

Dinner was a Caesar salad with a store-cooked chicken. Jenn couldn't bear the thought of cooking tonight after

31

the long day she had put in at work and wanted something easy to prepare.

Helping injured young soldiers every day was starting to affect her emotionally. Some needed to regain lost function in their arms and legs. Others were relearning to use whatever limbs they had remaining. The worst soldiers she encountered were those broken by their experience. Their eyes looked dead. When she peered inside, Jenn imagined she could see their soul lost in a dark territory between the past and the present.

There were too many soldiers still fighting the war even if they weren't facing the enemy. War was cruel. It stole young men's lives and bodies.

She prepared two plates and put them out on the table. If Anton didn't show up soon, she'd eat by herself, then take a shower and go to bed. Since they married in Las Vegas a couple of months ago, Anton's hours had become irregular, and Jenn wasn't sure when he would come and go. With a wine glass in her hand, she paced the apartment. She couldn't stop thinking about her day at work, the upsetting visit from the strange men, and Anton's inaccessibility.

As she passed the bookcase, Jenn stared at the pictures of their wedding. She looked happy in her rented gown. Jenn wondered when her happiness started to fade.

The sudden sound of a key turning in the lock made her jump. Anton strode into the apartment but didn't look at her. He rifled through the mail while he took off his coat.

"Did you have a rough day?" There was no welcoming tone in Jenn's voice.

"What?" he said distractedly.

"No 'Hi honey, I'm home?'" she said heatedly.

He pulled out an envelope. Jenn recognized the oversized shape. It was the account summary of her trust fund. Why didn't she put it away earlier? The money had become a source of contention between the two. Jenn had told Anton about it after they were married. Instead of accepting it as something she didn't want to touch, he kept asking her about it.

"What's this, babe?"

Jenn walked to her husband and yanked the envelope out of his hand. "Nothing important."

He cocked an eyebrow at her. "Are you keeping secrets?"

She scoffed. "One of us is."

"What does that mean?"

"Does the name Jimmy ring a bell?"

He blinked. "How do you know about Jimmy?"

"A couple of his friends dropped by. They said you needed to pay up fast."

"Oh," he said. Immediately the smug look on his face turned into one of concern.

"I'm sorry, sweetheart. They shouldn't have come here."

"Well, they did. Explain."

"Let me get you some more wine." Anton carefully took the nearly-empty wine glass out of her hands.

"I don't need wine. I need answers," Jenn snapped.

He quickly returned from the kitchen, holding a refilled glass. "You'll get both. Sit down."

Anton reached for the remote and turned off the television. He patted the seat cushion next to him. Reluctantly, she sat on the couch, allowing Anton to put his arm around her. He drew her close and gave her the wine glass. She didn't drink but held the glass between her hands.

"I told you things were bad in the business. It's worse than I said. I didn't want you to worry. Do you remember that I told you about my partner? I just discovered he embezzled all our joint funds, and he's fled the country."

"What?" Jenn sounded shocked. "When did this happen?"

"A couple of days ago."

"Did you report him to the police?"

"Yes, of course, but what are they going to do? The problem here is that someone started a rumor. People think I can't make payroll this week. Jimmy is the union shop steward and must have sent those guys to make sure everyone gets paid."

"Oh my god, baby," said Jenn. "How can you be so calm about everything?"

"It's why I haven't been around much the past few days. I'm definitely not calm. I've taken the time to wrap my head around everything and think about all my options. I'm screwed, and that's all there is to it."

"What happens now?"

"I have to find a way to finish the project, or I won't get paid. Unfortunately, the company is carrying so much debt that I can't get any new loans. I've tried. It looks like I'll have to file for bankruptcy."

Jenn gulped. A bankruptcy would affect their joint credit history. She had worked hard to build up her credit score. It was the only way she managed to live her current lifestyle. So many of her friends, like Nayla, didn't have a hope of getting an apartment on their own with their financial history. "That's awful. Isn't there anything else you can do?"

"There might be one thing."

"What?" Jenn had a sinking feeling in her heart.

"Let me borrow your trust fund money. I promise I'll pay back every dime once the state pays for the project. Including interest. It will keep my business afloat. It's really our business, because we share everything, don't we, sweetheart?" He gave her a kiss on the top of her head.

"I suppose we do," said Jenn weakly.

"The next contract will put the company solidly in the black."

"I don't know if this is a good idea."

He peppered little kisses on her neck. "It would help a lot. I wouldn't lose the business, and I'd have time to focus on the things that count."

"What things?" Jenn asked as he nibbled her ear, spreading heat through her body.

"My beautiful wife, for one thing." Anton found her nipple and gently squeezed it, making Jenn gasp.

"Okay. I'll get you the money tomorrow."

Anton hummed in her ear. "Let me show you how grateful I am."

CHAPTER 5

The Anquera sun brightly illuminated Emperor Kanton's packed audience hall. Shards of sunlight sliced through the floor from a skylight. On either side of the vast space, nobles and functionaries stood wearing brightly colored robes made from exotic fabrics. At regular intervals, imperial guards stood at attention in glistening armor.

When Kai and Commodore Bretland entered, they saw the Emperor sitting at a table plated with silver. The table brightly reflected its mirror finish. The Emperor's son, Prince Warrel, sat on his right-hand side. A small throne sat empty on his left. It was traditionally the position of the Empress, but since Kai's mother didn't have royal blood, she wasn't allowed to occupy the throne. The chair would remain empty as long as she lived.

On high court days, when Kai was at home, he stood at the Emperor's side. As the only member of the royal family currently serving in the military, Kai's presence was a symbol of the Emperor's total commitment to the fight.

On this day, Kai stood before the Emperor as a supplicant, not as a symbol. The Emperor sat on his throne and gazed at Kai and Bretland impassively.

Kai took the opportunity to study the Emperor's face, looking for any signs of stress. Few knew it, but Kanton injured his heart in a battle long ago, and it was weaker than normal. In private, the Emperor credited Kai's mother with giving him the strength to continue.

"Commander Imwaden," said the Emperor, "Thank you for bringing the enemy to our door with their proposal. We will consider it in session. Kai, join us while the guards take the Earth warrior to his quarters."

Kai sighed with relief. The Emperor did not use the title of hated enemy when referring to Bretland. He called him a warrior. It was a good sign.

Bretland looked at Kai questioningly but the Anquesh warrior, bound by court protocols, could not glance at him. Instead, he gave a brief nod of his head hoping to convey sentences in a slight movement. *It is normal, and you are in no danger*, Kai thought.

Kai wasn't sure if the Emperor would approve of the human's proposal. Bretland's claim that an Anquesh ally sought to weaken the Empire was not well-received by the nobles. It resulted in many angry looks. They expected deception from their enemy, not assistance.

Kai could only imagine what was going through the human's mind, and didn't have time to think about it. The Emperor expected him in the Council Chamber. He stepped forward, following his stepfather and the retinue of high advisors. Kai was the last to enter the room and found all the chairs at the long rectangular table occupied. Kanton motioned for him to step forward.

"You've brought us a proposal. I'm interested in your thoughts on the matter."

"I think we should consider it," Kai said slowly.

Immediately, the nobles at the table rose their voices excitedly. The loudest shouting was an argument against Kai's position.

The Emperor held up his hand. "I agree with Commander Imwaden. The war is getting expensive. Is everyone prepared to increase their tribute in support of the war effort?"

Immediately the nobles fell silent.

"I thought so," said Emperor Kanton. "We've discussed this issue to death before. While we would all give our lives for the Empire, no one seems willing to give their pocketbooks. The only question I have is how we would implement the agreement."

"Do we have a lot of choices?" asked Warrel. "The traditional way is best."

Kai studied Warrel carefully. He seemed a little too eager to insert himself into the conversation.

"You propose a marriage bond between one of our nobles and an Earth woman?" The Emperor stroked his chin. "Your idea has merit, but who shall we send? My brothers are either already married or too young. Warrel, you already have a marriage contract with Prince Renquel's daughter, so you're out of the picture."

"That's correct, Father."

"We can't insult our good servant Prince Renquel by refusing to join our houses together."

"There's an available bachelor at this table who is the proper age," said Warrel. "What about Kai?"

The Emperor turned toward Kai. "That's an idea."

"I'm not sure I'm worthy of such an honor," said Kai. Internally, he was beginning to panic. A human bride? From Earth? Absolutely not.

"Nonsense," said Warrel. His eyes glittered with enthusiasm for his new cause. "You're one of our strongest warriors. It should be easy to assert yourself over any female Earth sends us."

Others around the table murmured their agreement, and Kai saw in the Emperor's eyes that he would have to volunteer for the job, whether he wanted it or not.

"I believe we've settled the issue," said the Emperor. "We will propose a peace treaty based on a marriage between Kai Imwaden, son of the Royal Princess Andeleth of Anquera and any suitable female from Earth. I dismiss everyone except Kai."

Warrel smirked as he left the room. He looked satisfied that he had given Kai a terrible burden. The door guard closed the exit, leaving Kai alone with the Emperor.

"Thank you."

Kai did not expect to hear those words coming from the Emperor's mouth.

"I can count on a certain amount of discretion from you, and I appreciate that you didn't make a scene in front of my advisors about your task."

"I serve at the will of the Emperor."

"That's another thing I appreciate about you, Kai. You have a clearly defined sense of duty."

"I have to," said Kai. "I am well aware that the privileges I enjoy are because of your marriage to my mother."

"That's not entirely accurate. First, you've earned every single one of your privileges, and never let anyone tell you differently. Being my stepson has not made your path easier; on the contrary, every move you make is harshly scrutinized. Clan Imwaden has a long history of service to the Empire. You have never failed us. I want you to know that your mother has honored *me* in this marriage. She isn't merely my sindare, although that would be sufficient. She provides a frank and honest channel of wisdom. You have the same qualities. Let me run something by you. You suspect we cannot trust the Earth people's words, but you accept that this will provide us with a temporary cessation of hostilities. It will let us catch our breath."

"It's like you read my mind. Those are my exact thoughts."

"Your instincts are right. Don't tell anyone this, but I am personally negotiating with the Similcue. They are taking longer than expected. The Similcue are insisting on things I will never grant, but I think I'm close to an agreement."

"Are you sure we can trust them?" Years ago, the Similcue declared war against Anquera. The fighting ended with both sides calling the outcome a draw. Currently, the Anquesh and the Similcue tolerated each other but avoided each other's paths.

"With the support of the Similcue, we can easily defeat Earth and put that war to rest."

Kai didn't like the sound of the Emperor's statement, especially after Bretland's warning that another race was playing the Anquesh and the humans against each other.

"And you trust the Similcue?" Kai repeated.

"Of course not. I trust that they find a treaty with us advantageous. They're asking for a fortune in exchange for their aid. Until I have the Similcue on board, all you have to do is play along. When the agreements are signed, we'll pull out of the arrangement with Earth. I promise you won't have to marry one of them. I have another match in mind for you, and I'm sure she will be more to your liking."

Kai was shocked at the two pieces of information. The first seemed dishonorable. He could never imagine entering into an agreement under bad faith. And why was Emperor Kanton arranging a marriage for him? Kai didn't expect the act of generosity. The Emperor was heavily involved in the marriages of his brothers and son, but Kai wasn't related to the Emperor by blood. It should have been a great honor, but at this moment, Kai didn't feel special. He merely felt uncomfortable.

His mother had reminded him many times that being Emperor was not an easy job. It wasn't his place to second-guess the chain of command. "I will do your bidding."

"Wonderful. I'm giving you a new title for the assignment. You will be the official Emissary for this mission. I'll send you the papers before you leave. From this point forward, you are in charge. We'll give you diplomats for assistance and draft the agreement with Earth before you leave, with the usual provisions."

"As you wish, my lord." Kai wondered how he was going to explain to Bretland that the usual provisions included leaving Earth soldiers on Anquera as insurance.

"Thank you for your service. With your help, we'll conquer this damnable species."

CHAPTER 6

By the time Jenn reached her apartment, her head throbbed. Every muscle in her shoulders and neck was knotted rock-hard with tension. The first thing Jenn did after she locked her door was reach for the wine. The second was turn on the TV. She had to if she wanted to hear a human voice in the apartment. Anton was barely around these days. He hadn't even come home last night.

She had never remembered feeling this lonely. Today she needed him.

Anton, she thought. *Where are you?*

And in financial news, despite last week's reports of the advancing Anquesh fleet bringing their unexpected peace proposal, stock markets all over the globe continue to plunge. World leaders meet today in Oslo to discuss ways to shore up the global economy.

That was the last thing she needed to hear. She knew all about economic problems, just like all of her coworkers.

In a related story, the United Earth Alliance has signed a contract with the industry-leading interstellar matchmaking company TerraMates. TerraMates will lead the selection process for Emissary Kai Imwaden's prospective bride.

Jenn rolled her eyes and turned off the television. An Earth woman had to marry an alien? Ridiculous. She had watched a show which explained the marriage was an ancient Anquesh tradition, but Jenn thought aliens would have advanced far beyond such primitive beliefs.

Her phone rang. It was Nayla. Jenn felt like she had never been so happy to hear from her. Since her marriage to Anton, the two women rarely spoke.

"Hi, Nayla. I haven't heard from you for a long time."

Nayla ran her hands through her hair. "I'm sorry about that. You're going to think I'm a jerk for calling you like this, but I'm in trouble. Can I borrow some money? Things are getting bad now, and I lost my job."

"I'm sorry to hear that, but I lost my job too."

"You did?"

"Every dollar is going directly to the war effort, and they cut almost all the support services."

"I'm sorry."

"All I can do now is spot you fifty dollars."

"That would be great. I feel like such a bad friend. Only you would apologize for not being able to lend me money."

"Don't even think it. I understand. You're my sister, right? Whatever I have is yours. Unfortunately, it's not much."

"You're making me feel like a bitch."

"Come over. I'll make us some dinner."

Nayla paused. "Is Anton there?"

"He's out of town on business." Her statement was a lie, but she didn't expect Anton to come home soon, and she wanted to see Nayla.

"I'm not going to turn down a free meal. I'll be there in twenty minutes."

"Great!"

In the middle of Jenn's dinner preparations, the doorbell rang.

That was a quick twenty minutes. Jenn turned down the stove before she went to the door. But when she looked through the peephole, she didn't see Nayla. A strange woman stood in front of her door.

Jenn turned away. She wasn't in the mood for solicitors or Jehovah's witnesses. She turned back when the pounding started.

"Open up, Anton! You bastard!"

What was it now? thought Jenn in exasperation and anger. She unbolted the door and yanked it open so swiftly that the woman nearly fell inside the apartment.

"If you're with Jimmy, he already sent some guys. We know. We owe him money."

"I'm looking for Anton."

"Take a number," replied Jenn caustically.

The woman looked stylish in a gaudy sort of way. She wore her black hair in a short bob and slicked it back with gel. Her eyebrows were over-plucked, and her red lipstick was too garish for Jenn's tastes.

"When you see him, tell Anton his wife is looking for him."

"I know! I've been looking for him the past couple of days."

The woman looked down her pointed nose at Jenn, then stared at Jenn's wedding ring.

"Sister, unless you married him ten years ago, I'm his wife. You're just another woman on a long list of people swindled by Anton."

* * * *

Kai had seen death and destruction all over the universe, but that didn't prepare him for what he found on Earth. The humans created different types of technology that had nothing to do with combat. Each place he visited had something new that amazed him. One of the unique devices was a gift from the Earth government - an interpersonal communication device. Kai immediately assumed it was something from Earth's counter-intelligence division to spy on the Anquesh and was reluctant to use it.

He knew his handlers were only showing him the best Earth had to offer. Among all the outward appearances of wealth, there was tremendous poverty hidden beneath the surface. The Earth government didn't want the Anquesh to know the actual economic situation, but the Anquesh spies masquerading as diplomatic aides were adept at uncovering information.

What they found was appalling.

Many humans had no homes, no jobs, and lived on the street even though there was sufficient housing for all. Food was scarce. In some areas, there was rioting because people did not have enough to eat. Despite the plight of their citizens, nations still spent money to support the military. Kai knew his stepfather would never let conditions like this continue, which was why he was willing to entertain the notion of a treaty with Earth.

The biggest problem was that there were no noble houses to search for a suitable mate. The few royal lines which existed on the planet had no interested in joining with an alien. To fulfill Kai's request for appropriate mate selections, the United Earth Alliance contracted with a company called TerraMates, outsourcing the application process.

Dating was a concept foreign to Kai. In his homeland marriages were arranged. The groom and bride met in structured settings to learn about one another. Apparently the Earth women expected to be courted, taken to meals and other amusements. These activities were often unchaperoned. Kai thought it was ridiculous. He took what he wanted. Kai's diplomatic aides tried to explain that it was a matter of culture and that different societies have different customs. Humans did not have sindares.

Kai thought it sounded like a pile of shit.

Earth people, despite their free distribution of technology, were a peculiar and savage lot. He was now pleased with his uncle's plan, even if did carry the stench of dishonor. He wouldn't want one of these wretched creatures in his bed for a single night, let alone a lifetime.

Today he started touring the different facilities to evaluate the potential mates. Kai was not looking forward to it.

* * * *

Jenn woke with a jolt. Her sheets were wet with sweat, and the lights were still out in the dorm. The recurring dream had come again. It was a replay of the terrible night when she confronted Anton. In their acid-fueled argument, more of Anton's secrets came spilling out into the open. Anton had re-signed her lease on the apartment, and he drained every credit out of her trust fund. In both instances, he had forged Jenn's signature. It was a good thing she had Nayla there for moral support. Otherwise, she was so angry she thought she might have killed the dirty rat.

Nayla had dragged Jenn away and helped set her up at Nayla's grandmother's apartment. It quickly became apparent that Nayla had enough problems without adding another mouth to feed. In desperation, she signed up for the TerraMates Anquera program. As part of the new service, they fed and housed applicants while waiting for the selection process to end. Jenn was sure the aliens wouldn't select her. Many women had applied, but most didn't even make it through the TerraMates screening.

Women who could work, were in good health, and had a college education were considered good prospects. Jenn made the cut. She joined hundreds of other women at the Facility, a converted warehouse enhanced with makeshift bathrooms and a mess hall. Jenn's time in the Facility was like going to school all over again. Teachers gave lessons in the Anquesh language, culture, and manners.

Jenn found their language unintelligible and their culture barbaric. She was happy to blend into the crowd as long as she had a roof over her head. The chances of the Emissary picking here were minuscule. Many of the other women were gorgeous and loved the idea of marrying into their enemy's royal family.

The Facility was much better than starving on the street. After she had arrived, she discovered there was a two thousand credit stipend for women who weren't selected. The amount of money being spent was shocking, but Jenn supposed Earth needed the marriage to succeed. In her downtime, Jenn applied for odd jobs and crossed her fingers.

Today, after a shower and breakfast she went to her first class, Anquesh culture. But she was greeted with a surprise. At each seat at the table was a large, long box. The instructor, a middle-aged woman named Ms. Bellish, stood with a bright smile at the front of the class. The other potentials filed in and took their seats.

"Ladies, I have a surprise for you. Emissary Kai Imwaden is visiting our facility this week! The visit will be your chance to make a good first impression, so we've provided each of you with a lovely tailored dress and some heels. Get dressed and we'll see how you all look. No judging, ladies."

Jenn opened the box with her name on it. The dress was an emerald green, a color that looked especially good on her. She smiled. Even if she weren't selected, at least she would go home with some new clothes. As she imagined herself wearing the outfit, she idly wondered what would happen if the Emissary decided to choose her. Now that the moment was at hand, she couldn't imagine offering herself to an Anquesh monster.

She grabbed the box and went looking for a place to hide.

* * * *

At first, Kai had been excited to look through a group of beautiful human women, but now he groaned at the sight of the queue stretching in front of him. It was his third day at the Facility, and it felt like he had been here forever. TerraMates required him to spend a minimum amount of time with each candidate, no matter how flighty or vapid. The thought depressed him. There was nothing attractive about any of the women he had seen so far. Some were outwardly hostile, others fawned over him, and many of them touched him too freely.

At this point, he was tempted to pick anyone at random and take her back to Anquera to fight him in the marriage

51

ceremony. He knew his stepfather wouldn't let the situation progress that far. Kanton had asked Kai to draw the process out as long as possible while the emperor finished negotiations with the Similcue.

TerraMates staff set Kai up in an interview room, and the first woman of the day entered. Immediately the human threw herself at him. She seductively removed her top, sat on his lap, and kissed him.

"By the gods," he groaned. Kai didn't know how many more days he could take. He rose suddenly, dumping the woman on the floor. Without intending to go anywhere in particular, he ran down the hall, leaving his attendants in his wake trying to catch up with him. Kai was in excellent physical condition and outran them all despite the difference in gravity between Earth and Anquera. As he turned a corner, he ran into a dead end. He would be trapped again unless he found another way out. Every door in the hall was locked except for one.

With triumph, he flung open the door. It appeared to be a closet, but he didn't care. It would serve his needs.

Immediately he detected an intriguing scent. It was musky and a little bit sexy.

This planet is driving you crazy, he thought.

"Please go away," said a plaintive voice.

Kai's head whipped toward the sound. It sounded like music to his ears.

"Who are you?" As the scent overwhelmed his mind, he became obsessed with finding the speaker. He wondered about her appearance.

"I'm a nobody."

"Come here so I can see you, nobody." His voice had a husky tone, and he was surprised at its sound.

"No. Go away."

"I don't think so. Do you know who I am? I can do whatever I want here."

"What are you doing here?"

"Hiding from those unbearable women. But you? You're intriguing, Earth girl. I haven't even seen you yet, but for some reason I suspect you might be the most beautiful woman on whom I will ever lay my eyes."

"Oh, brother." Jenn sounded exasperated. "You lay on the lines thick, don't you?"

"I'm afraid my English isn't the best. What do you mean?"

"I need to get out of here." He heard a rustling noise and felt a shape trying to rush past him. With a sweep of his arms, he gathered the female to him, pressing her firmly on his body. Kai had never felt anything as good as her body against his, and he felt his cock begin to rise.

"Mine," came a primitive thought from deep inside his brain.

53

But Jenn would have none of it.

"Let go of me!" She struggled against his grip. Failing to free herself, she bit down on his arm. Kai gasped. She shot her knee up between his legs, making pain course through his body. He stumbled back and lost his grip. Jenn tore herself out of his arms and threw open the door. The sound of her fleeing footsteps echoed up the hall. Kai panicked at the thought that she might escape him.

Kai tried to move so fast that he stumbled as he lurched forward to run after Jenn. She looked back, fear in her beautiful eyes, and Kai resolved to take her fear away.

First he had to catch her.

He was about to overtake Jenn when they ran into a wall of people consisting of an Earth military escort, his diplomatic staff and the shocked faces of TerraMates representatives.

Jenn stood still, breathing hard, looking like a trapped animal.

"I've made my decision," said Kai. "I want this one."

CHAPTER 7

Jenn stared at the line of aliens and humans in front of her. *No way. Anyone but me.*

When she didn't say anything, someone else spoke up. "I believe the honor has paralyzed her," said Ms. Bellish, her TerraMates instructor.

"My lord," said one of the aliens. "Are you sure? You haven't even looked at all the candidates yet."

"Never mind, Aden. She's perfect."

Jenn found her voice. "No, I'm not. Far from it, in fact. I'm too fat. My legs are short, and my belly bulges. I have dry hair with split ends. My nails are chipped and cracked. See?"

She daintily held up her hand for inspection by the tall alien lord.

"Ms. Bellish," said an Earth military officer. "It was my understanding that *all* the women would be ready for the Emissary's inspection. Can you explain what happened? Why was this woman hidden in a remote part of the building when she should have been in line with all the others?"

"We haven't even been on a date yet!" cried Jenn.

"It doesn't matter. I found you and claim you according to our treaty. Anquesh don't date. I find it unnecessary. The search is over."

Jenn looked up at him, staring fiercely into his eyes. "It's not over. Let me tell you something."

"Ms. Carden." began a shocked Ms. Bellish, with a warning tone in her voice.

"Don't speak to my sindare in that manner," shot Kai. "If the human wants a date, then she shall have one. Prepare it!" He bent closer to Jenn, his breath close to her ear. "Get ready for our date. If the Earth people do not provide you with anything you need, ask for Aden, and he'll provide." He touched his lips gently to her neck. Jenn shivered as a sensual heat infused her body.

"Later," Kai whispered. He stood up straight. "Show me to my room."

The Emissary walked off with the other aliens and a United Earth Alliance officer. Jenn was left alone surrounded by a ring of humans.

"I can't do this." It wasn't clear to whom Jenn was speaking. "He made a mistake. Did you see him? He's monstrous. I didn't know how tall or how big he would be. The Anquesh are our enemy. No way. No fucking way."

"Miss Carden, you had plenty of time to think about the consequences of your decision before you decided to sign a contract. The decision of the Emissary is final. Your planet needs you. If you don't honor your obligations, we will arrest you for treason, and a military court will sentence you to execution."

"You've got to be kidding me. I didn't agree to that."

The TerraMates representative spoke up. "Yes, you did." Her usually cheerful voice was now stern. "When you signed the contract, you agreed to military service. You were told multiple times to read the agreement thoroughly."

Jenn shook her head, wondering how she could have been so stupid.

"Think of it this way," Sprague whispered. "If you don't do what the Emissary demands, Earth will be at war again. This time, Ms. Carden, the human race might not survive."

"Come on," said Ms. Bellish, gently taking Jenn's arm. "Let's get you ready. Is there any place you want to go? Your time on Earth is very short. It's time to speak up now."

Jenn closed her eyes and wished her nightmare would go away. When she opened her eyes, Ms. Bellish was still tightly holding her arm.

* * * *

There was a conversation going on around him, but Kai was barely listening to it. Instead, he flipped through the file provided by TerraMates. It was full of information on the captivating woman. From the instant he caught her scent, he could think of nothing else but possessing her. Kai was simultaneously delightfully ecstatic and terrified.

He couldn't get her face out of her mind. Kai saw her blonde hair and blue eyes everywhere he looked. His heart burned with the need to take her. And yet, even though he knew she must be his sindare, he remembered that Jenn looked unhappy when he made the announcement. Was she hesitant to marry an Anquesh warrior? She should feel honored.

"My lord, are you even listening to us?" said Tellen, the second of his diplomatic aides. Aden outranked him but had spent more time gathering information than attending to Kai.

"Yes, I was listening to your incredibly boring briefing," growled Kai. "It is possible I have something better to do with my time. Why do I have a team of aides if I need to make every decision myself?" Kai wondered if his bluster would provide a cover for his inattentiveness.

"Aden, please give me a moment alone with the Emissary." Aden nodded and left the room. Tellen spun around and raised a finger at Kai. "This human, Jenn Carden, is not even from the upper class of humanity."

"And what of it?"

"The Earth people are insulting you and Anquera by presenting you with such an ordinary woman!"

Kai roared, slamming down his hands on the table. "Remember your place, Tellen! When you speak of Jenn Carden, you are referring to my sindare. You will show her respect at all times. Don't forget yourself again. The next time you decide to overreach your position, I will know it is time to make sure your career in the diplomatic service is over.

Tellen stared at Kai. "Pardon me, my lord. I respectfully request you remember your mother's situation and how the court views her."

"How dare you bring my mother into this conversation. She is the Royal Consort. Do you not have any sense? Has the air on this planet affected your mind?"

"My lord," said Tellen with a resigned sigh. "I see you cannot be discouraged, and I have to approach this another way. I've been *fully* briefed on this mission. You cannot present the human at court as your sindare. She will not last a single day."

"What are you saying?"

"The humans have earned their status as *hated* enemies." Tellen paused briefly, looking Kai in the eyes to make sure he was listening. "We've never had an enemy that did so much damage to Anquera. Do you remember the incident at Calan Tourab? Our people will not stand for an alliance with the humans. They despise the idea of a treaty with these Earth people. If you install Jenn Carden as your wife and present her as your sindare, she will not be safe even if she never leaves your bed. Hatred for

Earth people runs deep in our blood. Don't you understand?"

"Of course I do. As a warrior, I felt the hatred myself. But a single human is not representative of the entire race. Jenn was not at Calan Tourab. I have found my sindare, and I will protect her. I refuse to do anything less."

"The issue is larger than the lives of two people," said Tellen. "Assassination is a natural tool for nobles to advance their political agenda. The Emperor understands this all too well. He knows what it's like to be a husband forced to protect his wife every second of her life."

"Be realistic. I know no one likes her, but I've never heard anything about her life being in danger."

Tellen sadly shook his head. "Multiple levels of security cover both you and your mother. I don't think you are aware of how hard we work to protect you. You've both been targets of multiple assassination attempts since your mother married the Emperor. You must start living in reality. She receives death threats daily. The Emperor's enemies believe that assassinating the Royal Consort would throw him into such a rage that all the nobles would no longer trust him. Now the peace proposal from Earth presents a new opportunity to spread rumors about the Emperor's competence."

Kai remained silent, wondering if Tellen's words were the truth.

"I only tell you this because you need to understand how vicious the nobility can be. This is why he did not expect you to go through with the marriage. Anquera will never tolerate an Earth woman a heartbeat away from the royal family."

Kai felt like his breath was being stolen from him as Tellen showered him with the details of Anquesh court intrigues. Petty court events weren't something he spent a lot of time thinking about. Kai's military career consumed his life. For him, court life consisted of an occasional party. Now he looked at Tellen in a new light.

"Who are you really, Tellen? I barely know you, and yet you seem to know intimate details of my life, my mother, and the emperor."

"You wouldn't know me, but I'm watching out for you. Your stepfather personally briefed me. I was assigned to protect and advise you on the correct decision. The Emperor cannot go through with this treaty if he wants to keep the throne. You need to control your emotions. We must continue delaying as long as possible until we can gracefully back out."

"How do you expect me to deny myself and live a lie?" Kai felt like life was rushing out of his body. The thought of being without his sindare squeezed his heart with crushing pain.

"My lord, we only ask you do to the same thing now that we do every day," said Tellen levelly. "You are expected to do your duty."

CHAPTER 8

Jenn requested two things for her date with the Emissary. The first was that they have dinner at Nardones. The second was that Nayla had to join them. When Ms. Bellish objected, she followed Kai's suggestion and contacted Aden. Ms. Bellish looked like she was sucking a lemon as she placed the call for Jenn.

"Of course," said Aden. "The Emissary's chosen can have whoever she wants at dinner. Fulfilling the request is not an issue for Anquera. Is it a problem for Earth?"

No one had bothered to inform Nayla about her appointment, so she was surprised when the military took her from her grandmother's apartment. Nayla stared at the two soldiers guarding her and Jenn with shock.

"Girl," said Nayla, "You don't play around when you want someone to go to dinner with you. Do you need me *and* the soldiers? You'd think one of us would be enough."

"It wasn't my idea to pick you up like that, Nayla," said Jenn apologetically. "I wanted to see you one more time before I got dragged off-planet for the war effort."

"I've looked at pictures of the Emissary. I don't think anyone's forcing you to go anywhere. Can you believe big, tall and hunky chose you? Do you think he'd take an extra woman with him? You know, in case you get tired."

"There's nothing funny about my situation. We're talking about my life. They're going to take me away to a planet millions of miles from here. I'll never see Earth again."

Nayla yawned as she sat on her hands. "I'll be honest with you. I don't see how this is a problem. It's not like you have anything keeping you here. I think it's a great adventure and a unique opportunity. If you marry into a royal house, would you be a princess?"

"I don't think so. Kai is considered a noble, but if I understand my lessons correctly, his title is equivalent to what we would call an earl on Earth."

"What's an earl?" Nayla was staring blankly off into space.

"It's a step below a duke. Princes, dukes, earls, that's how it goes."

"This is getting boring already. What would your title be?"

Jenn made an exasperated noise. "We'd say countess, but honestly, I don't know what they call it on Anquera. Is my title all you can think about? I'm going into the hands of the enemy. I'll be somewhere where I don't know anything or anyone."

"After we sign the treaty, they won't be our enemies anymore." Nayla was always practical. "Maybe we can get the economy going and there will be jobs for people again. I'm proud of you, Jenn. My best friend is going to be the reason Earth will fix itself. And I'll be right by her side."

Jenn swallowed hard. All she had thought about was herself and how she didn't want this kind of change in her life. She had never considered the impact of the treaty on billions of people on Earth.

This was too much responsibility. When did her life get so complicated?

When the seven foot alien with eyes to die for said that he wanted her.

Whoa. Where did that thought come from?

* * * *

"I am honored to meet your friend," said Kai. "Miss Nayla, you look lovely."

If it weren't for her extensive training, Jenn would have rolled her eyes. Kai seemed to have a cheesy line for every occasion. But she had to admit that Nayla looked spectacular. TerraMates provided her with a royal purple dress that highlighted Jenn's dark skin tone.

"Thank you, Emissary," said Nayla in the most polite tone Jenn had ever heard from her.

Jenn smiled to herself. Just who was she trying to impress? The Emissary of an alien planet, that's who. Not only was he royalty, everything about him, from his imposing size, runaway muscles, and long dark hair styled in dreadlocks dripped sex.

Kai wore a dark blue uniform jacket and white slacks. There was an unfamiliar crest over the left breast pocket of the jacket. He took Jenn's hand, which disappeared in Kai's large, warm palms. "Hello again, Jenn," he said in a husky voice.

"Hi." Jenn suddenly felt shy. This close, his imposing presence was practically overwhelming. She didn't know what type of cologne Kai used, but it was making her think about what it would be like to touch him.

She shook her head, hoping it would clear her thoughts.

Jenn said little during the limousine ride. In the meantime, Nayla and the Emissary chatted happily with each other. Nayla didn't feel any pressure and found it easy to be her usual bold joke-making self. She had to explain half of them because Kai's English wasn't the best. Jenn slowly became annoyed. It was apparent that the emissary was paying more attention to Nayla than to her.

"Girl! Aren't you listening to what your man said?" giggled Nayla.

"What?" As she thought about it, Nayla's playing up to the Anquesh man was bothering her. Of course Jenn didn't want him. Not really. She was obligated to be with him because she signed a piece of paper that she didn't understand.

They pulled up in front of the restaurant, flanked by a military escort. Someone had set things up ahead of time. The restaurant had no other customers, and the chefs had already prepared several pizzas. Jenn picked a table, and the owner brought over a selection of food.

"Is this restaurant one of your finest eating establishments? Someone took me to a five-star restaurant in Los Angeles."

"A Michelin-rated place? Sounds posh. What did you think about it?" Nayla asked.

"I'm not allowed to voice my opinions." Kai cast a quick glance at his staff standing just inside the door.

"Why not?" asked Nayla, practically squealing.

Kai leaned forward and lowered his voice. "It was awful." He gravely looked them both in the eye. "The women in Los Angeles looked like boys. They had no curves."

Nayla laughed. "You mean they were skinny?"

"They were so thin that I couldn't imagine how they sit on their asses without hurting themselves."

Nayla couldn't contain her laughter, which drew sharp looks from the people watching from the doorway. "You are a hoot, star man."

"Is that good?"

"It means she finds you amusing," said Jenn.

"I'll admit that it's enjoyable sitting with my chosen and her friend. It's unusual to get time for myself."

"Why is that? You don't get out of the palace much?"

"Jenn!" Nayla exclaimed.

The warrior flashed a concerned gaze toward Jenn. "Are you not feeling well? You seem unhappy."

"I'm fine," lied Jenn.

"She's just hungry," said Nayla. "When her blood sugar drops, she gets surly. If she's grumpy, it usually means she needs to eat."

"What is this food?" Kai picked up a slice of cheese pizza. Mozzarella dripped from the sides in strands.

"Pizza," said Jenn. "We consider it Italian food, but pizza like this is an original American creation." She paused thoughtfully. "I suppose you don't care much about our different countries."

"Not really. To me, you're all from the same planet." Kai gingerly picked up a slice. "Eat," he insisted, holding the food close to her mouth.

Jenn looked at Kai's hands like they were radioactive. "What are you doing? I can eat on my own."

"You honor me by accepting my offering. On my planet, one of the first things sindares do with one another is feed themselves."

Jenn started to blush against her will. "It seems a little intimate for a first date."

Kai cast a glance at the soldiers and staff lined up behind the front window, peering into the restaurant. "Usually, it is. It seems we cannot have any intimate moments. Let me try again." He carefully brought the pizza to her mouth a second time, and she reluctantly took a small bite.

"Tastes good. Perfect, in fact."

"Again." She found herself taking one bite after another. Jenn had to admit that there was something unexpectedly tender and touching about a huge warrior feeding her. There was a different kind of look in his eyes, something Jenn had never seen before in other men when they looked at her. His gaze seemed gentle and caring.

She didn't catch all of the last bits and a dribble of cheese slid down her chin. Simultaneously, they both tried to wipe it off her face, and Jenn laughed.

"You're making me feel ashamed. Let me take my turn." Jenn grabbed a slice and practically shoved it into the Emissary's mouth.

He carefully took a bite and a giant smile appeared on his face. "Humans aren't the best at fighting, but you might be the best at cooking." His grin, full of warmth, melted Jenn's heart to the consistency of the gooey cheese. Their eyes met, and Jenn could not pull herself away.

"It looks like you two could use some time by yourselves," suggested Nayla in a quiet voice.

"Unfortunately, that's not possible," said Kai. He sounded sad.

"Anything can happen when Jenn and I get together. The restrooms are down the hall."

"Restrooms?" said Kai.

"Yes. Work your way over there. I think I'll take a taxi home by myself." She pulled out her phone and winked at the couple.

"But Nayla, that's too expensive!"

"Don't worry about it. TerraMates spotted a couple hundred credits to my account for my trouble today. I consider it a donation to a good cause."

Nayla's phone beeped. "That was quick. It's here already."

"I don't understand," said Kai.

"I'll show you the way to the restroom, Emissary," said Jenn loudly, standing up and tugging at his arm.

"You do that." Nayla had a mischievous look on her face. "I'll wait here for you to come back. I'm prepared to wait a long time."

Kai followed Jenn even though he didn't understand her intentions. At the end of the hall was a metal door.

69

"We have to move quickly before our handlers realize we're starting a jailbreak." She opened the door and took his hand. "Let's go."

CHAPTER 9

Kai clutched his sindare's hand as she led him into an alley between two buildings.

"We shouldn't be doing this."

Jenn stopped suddenly. "You're right. We probably shouldn't. Do you want to go back?"

Kai looked into her blue eyes for a moment, then stepped back and gazed at the human speculatively. Everything about her was beautiful. Her presence triggered a fundamental desire to hold and protect her. At that moment, he was torn between his duty to his Emperor and the need to be with his sindare.

He'd read the poems and stories about what happened when someone found their sindare lovemate. He never imagined his feelings would be overwhelming. His heart pounded in his chest as he started thinking about touching her. Now that Kai had experience with sindare love, he understood why the Emperor's face immediately changed whenever he saw Kai's mother. Being with Jenn made Kai realize he had found a missing part of himself that he didn't know he lacked.

They expected Kai to give her up.

Impossible.

But keeping her would result in her death.

Perhaps they could spend a few precious hours together. Eventually, he would have to explain what Jenn needed to do to satisfy honor and put an end to this impossible mission. That way Jenn could walk away with her life. It would be painful for him, but she would survive.

"No," Kai said carefully. "I don't want to go back to the restaurant."

"Then let's move. The taxi's waiting and I'm sure the meter is running already." Jenn dashed away.

Kai slowly realized what the conversation about the taxi meant. He strode quickly to catch up with her as they moved out from the alley a few doors down from Nardones. He glanced at the small crowd of people waiting for them to come back from the restroom, but they all had their backs turned. Kai climbed into the car, and the vehicle started moving down the road.

Jenn was already settled into her seat and flipped down the control panel on the self-driving car. "Is there any place you want to go?" she asked.

The cab was cramped. Kai couldn't help but sit extremely close to Jenn. He breathed deeply, taking in her scent. He didn't care where they went.

"I don't know much about Earth. The one thing I know is that I want to be with you."

Her face flushed, and her fingers idly worked on the control board, pushing buttons at random.

"How can you be sure of that?" she asked. "We barely know each other."

"How can I not?" Kai's gaze swept over Jenn's beautiful body. Her skin seemed to glow and encouraged him to touch it. The swell of her breasts peeked out from the neckline of her dress. Kai wondered what it would feel like to lick them. He wanted to explore the curve of her creamy neck. Jenn's legs, barely covered by the short Earth dress, led his eyes from her petite feet up their graceful curves to the mysterious place between her thighs.

Everything about Jenn was delectable. Kai knew in his soul that they were destined for each other. Nothing in the universe would make him feel different.

With her overwhelming presence and his thoughts focused on the gorgeous exotic beauty, Kai's passion stirred and his cock swelled to an aching hardness. Kai was a soldier trained for discipline, order and duty. At this moment every fiber of his being cried out, needing to possess this woman. With a bold move, he engulfed her with his broad arms and bent his head to her lips. All his desire and longing came out in a fiery kiss. She melted into his arms as he pressed his lips to hers, taking her mouth with hungry kisses. He felt her heart hammer against his chest.

Kai's hand traveled below her waist. He pulled up the edge of her dress, using two fingers to lift the lacy fabric between her legs and caress the cleft of her fleshy mound. Jenn's breathing sped up, and she softly mewled as he explored her soft folds which were growing hotter and slicker with each stroke.

"Please," she moaned.

"What?" he whispered into her ear.

"Harder."

He found the sensitive bud in her cleft and smeared her wetness in and around it. She panted with her mouth open, and he kissed her again, this time penetrating her mouth with his tongue. Kai was knowledgeable about Anquesh sex, but he felt new sensations now that were more intense than anything he had experienced before. He slid his fingers into her hot channel and pumped them in and out while he swirled his thumb around her hard bud. She moved her body against his hand, her eyes going wide as he pushed his tongue further into her mouth, stifling her cries. Jenn wrapped her arms around Kai's neck, clinging to him as she moaned.

Jenn pulled back suddenly. "I never...I mean...I don't," she stammered. Her breathing and heartbeat slowed down. She pulled her arms away and smoothed her dress. She looked distressed, and Kai didn't understand why.

"Did I do anything wrong?"

"No. It's just...what must you think of me? We barely know each other, I feel like I'm representing the entire planet and I let you..."

"You're right." As Kai thought about the ramifications of what he'd done, he felt the cold chill of sobriety overtake his body. He drew back and sat upright. "I should not have touched you like that before I won your rights in the wedding ceremony battle. It was dishonorable on my part. It's my fault, and I apologize."

"It wasn't dishonorable. Definitely honorable. Kai, no one has ever cared enough about how I felt to take the time to...you know...bring me pleasure. Not like that. Um…what battle?"

He swallowed hard. A single question rushed to his brain.

"Other men have touched you?"

Jenn gave Kai a quizzical look. "Well, of course."

"Of course!" Kai's voice rose to a roar. "Who are they? I will challenge each one to battle!" It was *wrong* for other men to touch his sindare. Kai had never felt jealousy before in his life. The new and foreign emotion seized him with a fierce longing to prove that he was her mate, and no other.

"Emissary!" she gulped, drawing her body into the corner of the seat. Jenn was shaking. "Like a punching battle? You wouldn't do that, would you? What kind of aliens are you, anyway?"

"The kind of aliens that don't let other men touch their sindares!"

"Why do you keep calling me that?"

Kai gave a growl from deep in his throat. "It is the way of things."

"Maybe out there, but not here. People can and do have histories. Are you telling me you've never had lovers, Emissary? Should I hunt them down as well?"

He hated Jenn using his title instead of his name, and he didn't like her angry look. But her words had the desired effect, starting a calm flow of logic in his lust-driven brain.

What was the matter with him?

Is this what it meant to have a sindare? Would all his responses be outrageously exaggerated? Is this what other Anquesh felt when they met their sindares for the first time? It was a kind of madness.

Jenn was right. The thought of her with another man woke the battle urge in him, coiling in his gut, making him ready to strike. Of course he had lovers. But now Kai realized none of them had been important to him.

Jenn was important to him.

To make things worse, even though they shared a kiss that had shifted Kai's world, the look on her face suggested that she hated him. Jenn did not feel the same way toward him that he felt about her. Was she his sindare after all?

The thought crushed him. It brought him down fast and hard from his sexual high, like he was landing from a high-altitude jump without a parachute. The memory of Jenn's impending danger reasserted itself in his mind. If Jenn became his wife, her life was at risk. Kai could not allow harm to come to her, especially through his selfish actions.

He would not be able to marry her. Being with her now was futile.

"We are in an impossible situation," he said formally, falling back on his military training, the one constant in his life. "I respect your wishes in this matter. When the time comes for the marriage ceremony, I will not resist. You may defeat me in battle and honor will be satisfied."

"What the hell are you talking about?" Her voice rose to an ear-splitting pitch that hurt Kai's ears.

"It should be simple enough." Kai was angry at himself. To keep his rage under control, he bottled up his emotion. As a result, his voice came out cold and dismissive. "Since you will never be my wife, I will allow you to defeat me."

CHAPTER 10

Jenn stared at Kai. In an instant, he could switch from fervent passion to glacial coldness. She did not completely understand the alien or what was happening, but she knew one thing.

She was pissed.

Jenn was mad at TerraMates and the United Earth Alliance from keeping critical information from her. She was angry with Kai for toying with her feelings. Most of all, Jenn was furious with herself for allowing him to touch her intimately. He must think she was a slut or worse. That was why his attitude had changed.

"You'll have to explain everything to me."

"There is nothing further to explain." Kai's voice was hard, and his eyes looked off into the distance. "I told you. Should the time come, I will allow you to defeat me."

"I'm not going to fight you."

"I understand." Kai nodded his head. "If I immediately surrendered, you would be dishonored. You are correct. I should not treat a member of a worthy warrior race like they are unworthy. Very well, then. I will do my best to defeat you." Kai gave Jenn a wink.

"What?" she screeched.

"Does that not satisfy your honor?" Confusion spread across his face.

"I didn't have a problem with honor until you started talking about it. What is wrong with you people?"

Kai began speaking a string of words in Anquesh. Jenn assumed he was swearing.

"I do not know how to satisfy you then," he said frostily. "Take us back to the TerraMates facility."

Jenn shot him a cutting look. "Fine."

Kai stared straight ahead.

"If that's how you want it," she snapped.

He refused to rise to the bait and said nothing. Jenn programmed the destination into the car. Kai began to tap his fingers on his thigh, staring ahead, sitting stiffly in his seat.

But he was still close to Jenn, and his leg touched hers. A spark of passion moved into her core. She hated it.

Whatever cologne he wore drove her crazy. It was the sexiest scent she'd ever encountered. Now it was forever entangled with the crazy, passionate moment they recently shared and Kai's strange desire for combat.

She gazed out the window, looking for something to distract her. How could she have let herself get so carried away? With Anton, she hadn't done anything physical until a month after meeting him.

Jenn glanced at the side view mirror, a remnant from automobile designs of long ago. She noticed the same white car was always behind them. It seemed to be getting closer, but it wasn't moving into the other lane to pass.

"Is that vehicle one of yours?"

"What?" said Kai distractedly.

"The car behind us has been following this one since the restaurant. It's not Earth military. We use marked vehicles. Look at the side mirror."

"Are you sure?"

At that moment, their vehicle turned onto a ramp on the right. The other car followed suit.

"I'm pretty sure."

The taxi lurched forward. The vehicle following them accelerated to touch their bumper, causing the taxi to blink its lights and activate a siren. "Warning!" it blared. "Unsafe driving! This vehicle will report you to the police."

Jenn pulled out her phone from her pocket.

"What are you doing?"

"I'm going to sending Nayla a message. She can give our location to Earth's military."

"How can she do that?"

"We share our locations on our phones."

Jenn: SOS. Send help!

Nayla: For real?

Jenn: Someone's following us.

Nayla: On it.

The exit curved sharply to the left and descended from the raised highway to street level. The white car cut to the left and accelerated. As it moved next to the taxi, it shifted to the right and deliberately smashed into Jenn's car.

The crash flung Jenn into Kai's arms. He clutched her tightly as the vehicle skidded into the guardrail and spun around, stopping with a jolt.

"Get down!" yelled Kai as he pushed her to the floor. There wasn't any room in the tiny car, and Jenn found herself on her hands and knees, crouching against the crumpled door. She glanced up to see Kai with a weapon in his hand and an angry look on his face.

The side window exploded. Jenn quickly covered her head with her arms, closing her eyes. She heard an unfamiliar noise and realized it was Kai firing his alien weapon.

Police sirens pierced the air, and the gunfire stopped. Kai kicked out the door on his side of the vehicle and picked Jenn up like she weighed nothing, pulling her into the evening twilight. Lights flashed around them. A group of Anquesh appeared out of nowhere, along with Earth soldiers. The aliens quickly surrounded Kai and Jenn. He held her tightly wit one arm while barking out commands to the squad. The Anquesh leader looked unhappy but nodded his head. As a group, the Anquesh squeezed past the Earth Alliance military to the protests of Earth's commanding officer.

Kai shepherded Jenn into an Anquesh transport. Grim-faced Anquesh soldiers filed inside. When the aliens had filled every seat, Kai spoke to the driver and the vehicle sped off into the night. Kai remained standing, using his arm to steady himself. Jenn noticed a bluish-brown liquid dripping from his arm. With a shock, she realized Kai was injured. He wasn't looking at Jenn, and his expression was one of utter fury.

"Where are we going?" Kai ignored Jenn's question and she stopped asking. The oversized transport rattled down the highway, slowing down, bouncing and jolting as if it were traveling on uneven ground. The jarring ride unsettled Jenn's stomach. The Anquesh warriors, including Kai, stared straight ahead, not showing any reaction.

She had never felt more alone than among this group of aliens.

When the transport stopped, the door immediately opened. The soldiers stood and filed out the door, holding their weapons at the ready.

Before Jenn knew what was happening, Kai appeared in front of her and lifted her out of the seat.

"There's not enough time to explain. You'll have to trust me." To punctuate his words, he gently pushed her through the door.

Jenn stepped out of the transport to find herself surrounded by the Anquesh warriors once again. Kai stood behind her and shouted something in an alien language. The soldiers advanced, and stepped double-time through a field. A looming dark shape rose in the distance. She couldn't see the details, but she could tell that the object was huge, whatever it was. As they approached, a sliver of light appeared in the darkness. The soldiers parted slightly to form an aisle in their midst. Kai took Jenn's hand, pulling her up a walkway and into a huge room that looked like the interior of a warehouse.

One of Kai's diplomats was waiting for them. He stepped forward and put his fist to his chest. By his demeanor, it seemed that this alien was no mere ambassador. There had been so many soldiers present during the TerraMates training that Jenn was able to recognize a military man.

How much have the Anquesh deceived us? Jenn thought.

Kai and his diplomat had a quick exchange in Anquesh. The group of soldiers dispersed and two minutes later, Kai and Jenn were alone.

"There's time now to explain what's happening, I assume."

"Not yet." Kai's eyes narrowed. Without warning, he grabbed her and swung her onto his broad shoulders. As she started to kick and yell, Kai started walking purposefully through different corridors.

Jenn felt sick when she realized they weren't in a building. They were in a spaceship.

"Let me go!" she screamed.

Kai ignored Jenn's demands as he took her down an elevator. He stopped in front of a depression in the wall. The seam of a door appeared and opened, revealing a room barely larger than a cubicle. It contained a single platform for sleeping and an inset workstation in the wall with a chair.

Kai deposited her on the bed unceremoniously.

"The toilet is on the left. I'll need your hand for a moment." Jenn silently rose from the bed. Kai took her palm and pressed it firmly against a wall panel. The warrior muttered some words, and a mechanical voice answered him.

"You are now keyed to use the services in this room."

"How does that help me? I don't speak Anquesh."

"Good point," he said gruffly. "Computer, use Earth language protocols in this room. Change the security level to basic."

"Yes, Commander Imwaden," a mechanical voice responded.

"Commander? Not Emissary?" said Jenn.

"Now we're on my ship, the Ruvien," Kai said firmly. "I'm the commander of the vessel. We are on our way to Anquera."

"Hold on a second. I didn't ask to get thrown onto an alien ship and go on a ride through interstellar space."

"No, Jenn Carden, you did not." Kai turned and left Jenn to think by herself.

LISA LACE

CHAPTER 11

By the time he made it to the medical bay, Kai could barely walk. Some called it battle rage. The Anquesh called it nuxmunit. It began with the attack on the car, but it was fading now, and he was starting to feel weak.

By the gods, he thought. *Who attacked us?*

He ran through the possibilities in his mind. Was it someone from Earth, such as the military or a terrorist organization? A faction from Anquera looking to destabilize the government? Or was it a third race, biding its time and waiting for the most opportune moment to strike?

"Commander!" The medical tech was surprised to see Kai. "I need help. The commander is wounded."

Others rushed to Kai's side. In his depleted state, the faces blurred together, and he couldn't recognize anyone. He started swaying on his feet. Someone led him to a bed, lifting him up and helping him sink into the comfortable pad.

The doctor examined Kai's body, taking note of his multiple wounds. He had bruises on his shoulder, upper arm, and right chest.

"Did someone beat you up? What weapons cause injuries like these?"

Kai laughed. "They were using bullets. Earth weapons."

The doctor made a derisive noise. "How primitive."

"It doesn't matter how the target dies, as long as they stay dead." Kai held back a groan that lingered in his throat as the doctor began to prod his body.

"We need to take them out."

"You don't need my permission to do your job." Kai's patience was at an end. Not only had his security failed to provide information about a possible attack, he was also forced to bring Jenn onto the Ruvien for her protection. Without knowing the identity of the attackers, it wasn't safe to leave Jenn in the hands of Earth's military forces.

Kai had been shocked at how easy it was to slip away from the people who were assigned to protect them. Neither the Earth Alliance troops nor his handlers should have let the situation deteriorate to the point where a flight was necessary. Aden never made it back to the Ruvien once Kai sounded the evacuation order.

The only explanation that made sense was that Kai had a spy among his men. His lack of vigilance and over-reliance on his people had put both him and Jenn at risk. Now he wasn't sure who to trust. It was a bitter pill to swallow, and he wasn't going to make the same mistake twice.

The doctor administered local painkillers, but it still hurt when instruments poked around in private places. Kai kept his eyes fixed on the ceiling, doing his best not to show weakness. The doctor seemed enthusiastic about digging his instruments into Kai's body. The crude Earth bullets made a clinking sound as the medic dropped them into a metal pan.

"Save those," said Kai. "I want to analyze them later."

"Yes, commander."

The medic gently wiped away the blood from Kai's body and squeezed gel into each of the bullet holes. Kai was familiar with the treatment. The gel gave a short-term anesthetic effect while helping to heal tissue. When the doctor finished applying the gel, he laid strips of artificial skin on the wounds.

"Sorry to tell you this, but you can't exercise or shower for a week."

Kai raised his eyebrows. "That seems like an excessively long time."

"If your temperature rises or these wounds start bleeding again, come back here immediately. If you don't, I'll make sure your record shows you disobeyed your doctor's orders."

"Got it." Kai tried to sit up but shook his head. The room was spinning around him.

"No way." The doctor pushed him back down on the bed. "You have to rest here while we monitor your vital signs. We won't release you until we're sure you are well enough to walk."

Before Kai could reply, two figures walked to his bed. It was Tellen and his second-in-command, Lieutenant Sevit.

"Commander," said Tellen. "We have no new intelligence about the attack. The United Earth Alliance denies any involvement. They are also agitated that you took the woman. They demand her release."

"They can demand all they want. I'm not returning her."

"Sir, is that the most diplomatic solution?"

"Just a minute, Tellen." Kai held up his hand. "Sevit, take these bullets to security. Ask them if they can learn any new information."

"Sir, they would likely need assistance from Earth. The same people you plan to blow off about Jennifer Carden."

"Just tell the United Earth Alliance we expect their full cooperation to find the criminals who attacked me and my sindare."

At Kai's last words, Sevit raised an eyebrow.

"Are you waiting for something, Lieutenant? I gave you an order."

"Yes, sir," said Sevit crisply. He picked up the pan that held the bullets and left.

"What are you going to do with the Earth woman?"

"That is my business, and mine alone."

89

"The Emperor will disagree."

"I couldn't leave her there by herself. For all we know, her government's been compromised. I had to decide which one was the greater evil: leaving her with her own people or bringing her to ours. If she's with me, I can oversee her protection. It's my duty as her sindare."

"Sindare." Tellen shook his head. "How can you know? You need to test your assumption in combat."

"Have you found yours?"

"I am an old warrior. It's unlikely to meet my sindare at this stage in my life. I am quite satisfied with my wife."

Kai knew that if Tellen found his sindare, he wouldn't talk lightly about them. An ordinary woman would never invoke the depth of feeling that the Earth woman had aroused in Kai.

"Regardless," said Tellen. "The problem still stands. You cannot present Jennifer as your sindare to the emperor."

"I know. But allow me the dignity of making sure she is safe."

"And how do you propose to do that with the current political climate?"

Kai didn't know.

* * * *

Jenn paced around the little room, her ire gathering into a ball of anger.

"How dare he!" she muttered. "He thinks he can kidnap me, imprison me in a room and leave me alone, damn it!"

"Is there a problem?" A voice with a slightly mechanical tone echoed through speakers hidden somewhere in the walls.

She felt silly talking without seeing anyone, but she wouldn't let her discomfort stop her. "Where is the Emissary?"

"Sorry. I do not understand your question."

"Oh, great," groused Jenn. The last thing she needed was a computer that didn't understand her. "Let me try a different query. Where is Kai?"

"Do you mean Commander Imwaden?"

"Yes. Are there a lot of Anquesh named Kai around here?"

"Commander Imwaden is unavailable. Do you want me to leave him a message saying you want to see him?"

"No!"

"Very well."

Jenn didn't think that was what she wanted. She needed some answers. Was the Anquesh Emissary the only one who could give them to her? How long would it take?

"Wait, I changed my mind. Yes, I do want to see him."

"I will relay the message. One moment. It appears that Commander Imwaden is not on the active duty roster."

"What does that mean?" Jenn clenched her teeth.

"Not only is Commander Imwaden unavailable, but he also is not currently receiving messages."

"Let's try something else. I want to speak to someone that *is* available."

"I will relay the message," the mechanical voice said. "I have notified Lieutenant Sevit that you wish to speak to him. He will be here in approximately thirty minutes."

"Thirty minutes!"

"I detect a high level of stress in your voice. Do you have physical needs that warrant attention?"

The phrase 'physical needs' made Jenn flash back to the car where Kai did delicious things to her body. She had to shut her thoughts down. She was on an enemy alien ship, and she didn't want to think about sex, especially when a machine triggered the memory.

"No, I do not."

"Are you certain? Do you require food?"

The rumbling in Jenn's stomach told her yes. A single slice of pizza hours ago was hardly enough to keep her going. When she didn't answer right away, the computer didn't wait for her. "I will put in an order to the kitchen for you."

A buzzer sounded. "Per your request, Lieutenant Sevit is here to see you. Shall I open the door?"

"Yes." Jenn paused a moment. "Thank you."

An Anquesh warrior walked in with a wary expression in his eyes. He began speaking in Anquesh. "Lieutenant Sevit does not speak English or Standard," said the computer. "He ordered me to translate. The Lieutenant asks what you want."

Jenn glared at the man who towered over her.

"Where is Kai?" she demanded.

"The commander is unavailable."

"The computer told me that. I'm looking for more information. If he's not available, where is he precisely? I assume he's not lost in space." Jenn's words came out more fiercely than she had intended.

Sevit spat out a few words. "Commander Imwaden is in the medical bay. The staff is treating the wounds he received on your planet." The computer's mechanical voice did not have the same coldness that came from the Anquesh warrior's mouth.

"Oh. Is he going to be okay?"

"He will live. The Commander's health is not your concern. You've done quite enough already. Is there anything else you require at this moment?"

The Lieutenant's tone implied Jenn was the cause of his commander's injuries. She supposed she was, from a certain point of view. If she hadn't encouraged Kai to run away from the restaurant, the ugly mess would never have happened.

She shook her head no.

"Sleep pleasantly." The door closed as Sevit left the room.

CHAPTER 12

Jenn had fallen asleep. When she jolted awake, the lights in the room were off. The room was dark except for some light streaming in from the hallway. A hulking figure stood at the entrance.

"Turn on the damn lights!" Jenn shouted. The tiny room lit up, and she could finally see who was waiting for her outside the door.

It was Kai.

She gulped. He had one hand against the doorframe and his pose highlighted his sculptured body. Kai had changed his clothes. Currently, he wore a uniform with a metal breastplate which left his muscular arms uncovered. Unconsciously, Jenn stared at him, trying to get the memories of his hands out of her mind.

He didn't move, and Jenn quickly became impatient again. "Are you going to come in?"

"I was just checking on you."

"Why would you do that? Do you think I'm going to wander off unsupervised? You're holding me against my will. I'm sure your computer is keeping excellent tabs on me. You must want something else."

Kai looked away. He was trying to figure out the correct response.

"Well?" demanded Jenn. "Do you have anything to say for yourself?"

"No. A warrior does not need to explain himself."

"You jerk!" She flew at him, her frustration at her situation pushing her to recklessness. Jenn hammered his breastplate with her fists. "How dare you take me from my planet! How dare you imprison me!"

Kai's face looked pained as he easily pulled her fists away from his chest. With a sigh, Kai pushed her back into the cabin, this time moving inside and closing the door. He started talking, enumerating several points with his fingers.

"First of all, I'm the commander of this ship. It reflects poorly on us if you make angry displays where the crew can hear you. Second, I'd appreciate it if you didn't hit me. My wounds are still healing, and the medical officer will give me a bad report if they start bleeding again. Finally, I brought you onto my ship because I wasn't sure who was trying to kill us. It's possible that you have become entangled in Anquera politics. If someone tried to kill you because you were with me, it's a problem. I understand that you want nothing to do with me, and I respect your decision."

"Where did you get the idea that I want nothing to do with you?"

"You were angry with me in the taxi when I touched you. You were right. It was unworthy of you and dishonorable of me."

Jenn stared at Kai. She could hardly believe a word she was hearing.

So he does think the worst of me, she thought. *I'm stuck on a spaceship with a space hulk who thinks I'm a slut.*

"I won't bother you again."

* * * *

Kai couldn't forget the angry look on Jenn's face as the door slid into place, separating them again. He hung his head. His sindare hated him, and for good reasons.

It was foolish for him to come back to her cabin. He had lied to himself. He didn't need to check on her at all, but he wanted to see her. He needed to touch her, even if she didn't want him.

For the first time in his life, he had no idea how to get what he wanted.

Kai thought he could stash Jenn on a backwater planet somewhere and keep her away from danger, but he realized now it was foolish. She would be just as unhappy there as she was on Anquera. She wanted to go home. If their situations reversed, he would want to back too, regardless of the danger.

He felt the room sway around him for a moment, then remembered the doctor had threatened restriction to the medical bay if he didn't get some rest. He made his way down the hall to some temporary quarters he had co-opted from a junior officer and fell into the bunk. It wasn't as comfortable as his, but then again, the junior officer didn't have the Princess of Anquesh as a mother. She had pulled some strings to bring in another mattress and other conveniences to make her son as comfortable as possible.

Maybe it was the pain of his injuries, or maybe the pain from believing his sindare hated him, but Kai gave into the urge to call the one person who would understand his feelings.

The screen on the wall shimmered, and he saw his mother standing in a garden with the Anquera night sky behind her.

"Son?" said Andeleth, her face and voice filled with concern. "Are you well? You never call me when you're in space."

"I'm doing fine...er...how is the emperor?"

Andeleth's eyes narrowed. "I know you well. Don't bother hiding behind inquiries about my husband's health. You know I watch him every minute. You never contact me without a reason. What is the purpose of this call?"

Kap paused. "I have met my sindare."

"That's fantastic!" Andeleth's sudden expression of joy slowly gave way to consternation. "Wait. Is it an Earth woman?"

"Yes," said Kai miserably. "And she does not desire me."

The princess clucked. "That's considerably less wonderful. I don't believe you. Who wouldn't want my handsome son?"

"Mother," protested Kai. "Even if she did, it presents problems, and you know it. You've hidden many things from me."

Andeleth raised her head. "I didn't want you to worry."

Kai frowned at his mother's admission. She had known she was in danger and didn't share it with him.

"Tell me about her," urged Andeleth, trying to change the subject. "Is she pretty?"

"I can't get over her hair. It's a combination of gold and yellow hair."

"Gold! I don't believe it."

"Her eyes are as blue as the dress you wore at Hanton's wedding."

"Really? So you consider her exotic."

"Very much so. She would be an excellent prize for any warrior."

"Of course. But how can you be sure she is your sindare?"

Kai felt his cheeks flush, and he tried to look away before his mother saw his face.

"Ah," said Andeleth knowingly. "You took liberties with her already."

"It wasn't like that," protested Kai. "It was something special. I didn't know that the mere act of touching her would make me feel completely different."

"Sometimes it will, especially if the bond is very strong. I speak from experience. I knew Kanton was my sindare when we met at a court party. He took my hand and I was never the same again. Tell me something. How can you function right now when you are not with her?"

"I told you," Kai growled. "She does not want me."

"It sounds impossible if your bond is as strong as you claim."

"I dishonored her by the way I touched her. She is angry with me."

"So it was like that after all."

"That isn't the point," said Kai exasperated. "What should I do? I'm trapped in an impossible situation."

"And how is that?"

"I thought the Emperor didn't keep anything from you." Kai's voice came out in an accusatory tone, and he immediately regretted it.

"The Emperor and I have faced many challenging situations over the years. He couldn't imagine you would find your sindare among the Earth savages. Now that your situation has changed, I'll have to convince the Emperor that we should adjust our position."

"It might not be as easy as that. Tellen says having an Earth woman a heartbeat away from the royal family is intolerable."

She hissed. "Tellen is not trustworthy, no matter what your stepfather believes. He finds a way to be on every side of an issue. Let me worry about Tellen. I will talk to the emperor. We will make sure your sindare is welcome among our people."

"Bringing her was never the issue. The question is, will she be safe?"

Andeleth smiled. "Spoken like a true sindare. I cannot promise her safety, my son. That's your job."

"First things first. How can I get her to accept me?"

Andeleth shrugged. "Do you remember the kitith you tamed as a child?"

Kai had forgotten about the wild creature. It lurked in his garden outside his room, stealing food from Kai's plate when he wasn't looking. Eventually, Kai trained the animal to take food from his hand.

"If you could tame that kitith, you can tame an Earth woman. You'll figure it out. I will be glad to see you when you return home."

Kai sunk back, letting his head hit the pillow. It was good to talk to his mother, but somehow his problems seemed worse than before. He needed to make Jenn see that they belonged together. And he suspected Jenn would be more difficult to tame than a wild animal.

CHAPTER 13

Jenn paced the floor, waiting again for Kai to show up at her room. It felt more like a prison cell. For the past few days, he would appear at random times, talk to her briefly, then leave again. She was getting tired of the routine. He would say nothing of significance and never answered her questions.

It didn't help that she had drop-dead sexy dreams of the Anquesh warrior. As soon as she closed her eyes, she found herself in his arms again. He was all over her body, stroking, licking, and kissing. But the Kai of her dreams was vastly different from the stern warrior who visited her every day. Why did she keep hoping that the alien she dreamed about was real?

It was crazy, and she knew it. Despite his claims of protecting her, she was a prisoner on a spaceship. Perhaps they were going to use her as a hostage. Kai might think she was a bargaining chip. If that was the case, Anquera was in for a big disappointment. Jenn wasn't important enough to be valuable to anyone.

Today she decided she was getting some answers, whether he wanted to give them or not.

The door chime sounded. Kai entered the room, holding a bag. He looked at her warily. Good. She felt angry enough to spit nails.

"Are you distressed?" he asked cautiously.

"Distressed? I don't know, Commander. How could I be distressed with these lovely accommodations?"

As usual, he ignored her jibe.

"Soon we'll arrive at Anquera. I brought you a change of clothes."

"What's wrong with the dress I'm wearing now?"

"Well, you've worn it for five days."

Jenn looked down at herself. Her dress was looking wrinkled and a little worse for wear, but she had tried to keep it clean.

"I wash it each night," she protested.

"Yes, and I appreciate that. But your dress shows your legs, and that isn't the style on Anquera."

"The aliens are particular about the type of clothes I wear," said Jenn acidly.

"Exactly. I'm glad you understand," said Kai firmly. "You'll be meeting members of the court and it is important to conduct yourself properly."

"I'm not proper enough for you?"

Kai sucked in a breath. "You are the second Earth representative to appear before the Anquesh court. You will be the first woman. It is best for your world and mine that you make a good first appearance."

"I thought I was special before, but I feel considerably less special knowing that I'm the second. Who was the first?"

"Commodore Bretland."

"He's alive? Everyone on Earth thought you executed him." This was the first good news Jenn had heard for a long time, and it gave her hope.

"Of course he's alive, along with his battle group. They are enjoying Anquesh hospitality."

"Just like me, right?"

"Gods," said Kai, his eyes flashing. "Do civil words ever come out of your mouth?"

"Occasionally. But I might be finding it hard to be civil at this moment."

Kai moved on her quickly, clasped her shoulders, and looked down. His dark eyes bored into hers. "You will always be in danger on Anquera. You will be in less danger if members of the court can see you as a real person instead of the primitive creature in their imaginations. Most Anquesh think of everyone on Earth as a hated enemy. It is important for you to understand this. We are talking about hatred, not honor. If we honor our enemies, we will welcome them to our tables when we defeat them. If we don't..."

The Anquesh warrior stared at Jenn so intently that she felt like shriveling away from his gaze. But Kai's words lit a spark inside her. *Savage? Hated?*

She wouldn't give him the pleasure of seeing her back down.

"At least my people aren't kidnappers," she snapped.

"No," he said coldly. "They are murderers. Is that better?"

"Murderers!"

"Do you remember what happened at Calan Tourab?"

"Now you're talking nonsense."

"Calan Tourab is the gas giant where we first encountered the people of Earth. We were only a small trade convoy, but when we made first contact, your military destroyed them all. Those people weren't warriors, Jenn. You slaughtered them all and earned the wrath of every Anquesh citizen in the process."

Jenn looked away. Was Kai telling the truth? Did humans fire the first shot across the bow of the Anquesh war machine?

"I had nothing to do with that," she stammered.

"Do you think that matters? On Anquera, you're a representative for everyone on Earth!"

There it was again, an all-consuming responsibility for her people that threatened to consume her whenever she was in Kai's company. The worst thing was that she could tell he thought awful things about her. To the Anquesh commander, she was a slut as well as a murderer. She knew this alien warrior did not find her desirable. She lowered her head.

"I can see now why I'm not a suitable wife for you," Jenn said sadly. "But I'm not a savage, despite what your people think. Give me the dress and I'll show you."

* * * *

When Jenn exited the Ruvien, more people were watching than when she entered. She walked down a gangplank between two rows of huge Anquesh honor guards. The path lead to a small group of elegantly-dressed people standing on a raised platform a few hundred yards from the ship. A crowd of people cheered when Jenn and Kai came into view, and they didn't stop cheering until the pair reached the platform.

With one hand on Jenn's shoulder and another on her elbow, Kai gently urged her up the stairs that were a few inches too tall for Jenn. The height made her feel clumsy as she made her ascent, but Kai supported her, so she didn't have to look graceless. A hot breeze made the overhanging flaps of the tent flutter. Everyone on the platform had a solemn expression on their faces.

At the top of the platform, Kai moved to her side and bowed to two people in the middle of the group. From their clothes and elaborate headdresses, it appeared that they were the Emperor and his princess. The Emperor was an imposing figure and the princess at his side looked delicate and elegant. Jenn had to stop her mouth from dropping open at the aliens' majestic aura. Everyone was two heads taller than her, and she felt like a child again.

Kai silently squeezed her elbow and Jenn remembered his rushed instructions. She bowed at her waist.

"Your highnesses, I present to you Jennifer Carden, from Earth, their candidate for marriage. She is my sindare."

Jenn thought she could hear the intake of breath from some people on the dais, but it was very faint. Perhaps it was the wind.

The air hung thick with anticipation as the Emperor inspected Jenn. His eyes traveled up and down her long gown.

"Rise, Kai Imwaden, and Jennifer Carden from Earth." The Emperor said nothing else, but the woman at his side moved forward and held out her hands. Jenn took them and the woman warmly smiled.

"Welcome you to Anquera. My son has told me about you. I look forward to spending time with you and learning more your planet."

Jenn couldn't help but smile back. The woman seemed warm and genuine, and Jenn thought she might be a friend.

"I am honored. Kai didn't tell me his mother was gorgeous."

The woman chuckled, and the Emperor cracked a small smile. "That is the way of sons, isn't it? He has not failed to tell me how beautiful you are. It's good that he didn't try. Words would not adequately describe your appearance."

Jenn felt dizzy from the compliment. She wondered if his mother was making a show for the sake of the audience. She didn't believe that Kai told his mother she was beautiful.

Jenn didn't have much longer to feel good about herself. In the space of one breath, a roar sounded. A section of the tarmac rumbled as it split and sprayed into the air. People in the crowd began to scream, scattering themselves and finding cover. Guards rushed up the platform and pulled people off the dais, starting with the royal couple. Jenn didn't have time to think about what to do.

Kai swept Jenn into his arms and looked frantically for a way off the platform. People jammed the stairs. He lifted her up in his arms and jumped down. Landing with a roll on the tarmac, Jenn was trapped by his arms and pressed against his body as they made several turns. Kai stood in a swift motion, hauling Jenn to her feet, but he wasn't fast enough. Another roar rose above the clatter and screams. The ground shook as the sound of an explosion filled her ears.

The last thing Jenn remembered was falling forward.

109

CHAPTER 14

Jenn heard Kai shouting. "I don't care! Leave the Anquesh translator on as long as she's here."

"Your proposal is irregular," said another voice.

"She is my sindare. Jenn must have the ability to understand the language."

"What is going on?" She groaned, fluttering her eyes open.

"Lie still, Jenn," said Kai. "You have a nasty injury on your head. Our doctors aren't sure how to treat you since they don't know human physiology."

"Aren't you keeping a bunch of our ships hostage? Bretland has doctors, doesn't he?"

"Even while injured, she can give you a good suggestion. Yes, sindare," Kai said, his voice softer than usual. "That is an excellent idea. Someone call Bretland's battlegroup and speak to one of their doctors."

"Do you mean me?" The man sounded horrified.

"If you don't, I'll have someone else replacing you within the next ten heartbeats."

"Yes, my lord. But what about your injuries?"

"I'll manage."

Jenn turned her head to look at Kai again. This time, she noticed streaks of blood staining his handsome white uniform and silver breastplate.

"Are you hurt?" she asked.

"A little bit, but not like you. Apparently my head is harder than yours."

He deadpanned his last line, but she smiled despite his alien attempt at humor. Jenn coughed as a flash of pain shot through her head and ribs.

"You have to get some rest."

"I'm sure I'll be okay. What happened?"

"Someone started dropping bombs on us. We don't know who is responsible yet. Security is trying to learn more. The devices were crude."

He spoke without emotion. Did Kai really have no reaction to the violence they had just experienced? When she thought about how close they came to death, Jenn started trembling again.

The doctor returned. "I have the chief medical officer from Earth's flagship on a secure communications channel."

"Good," said Kai. "If you have difficulty understanding the translation, feel free to ask me. I am becoming proficient in English."

The doctor's face came on the screen at the foot of Jenn's bed. The Earth doctor asked Jenn some questions about her pain and how she felt. Upon request, the Anquesh medical staff provided images of Jenn's internal organs, passing a scanner over her body. The results displayed on one side of the Earth doctor's screen. The doctor stared at the images for a moment.

"You got lucky. It looks like you only have soft tissue damage. Jenn, you'll be sore, but your bones aren't broken. You appear to have a mild concussion. Someone will have to watch over you and wake you every two hours."

"We'll take care of it," said Kai.

"I'd feel better if I could examine her in person, of course."

"I'm sorry. That will not be possible."

"Call me if you have any questions. You know where I am," said the doctor, shrugging his shoulders. Jenn understood what was happening. They were trying to get her onto an Earth ship, but the ruse didn't work. Maybe Earth was planning a rescue operation for her. She hoped somebody was. Knowing humans were hated enemies made her worry even more about being in Anquesh hands.

"Doctor," said Jenn. "Are you and your men okay?"

"We're protecting them," said Kai. "I will permit no further questions on this topic, and I will verify their safety myself."

"Jenn, can you get information on Commodore Bretland? We haven't seen him since he left with the commander."

"He is enjoying the hospitality of the Anquesh Empire, and that is all you need to know," said Kai. He made a motion in the air with his hand, and the communication ended.

Kai turned to Jenn. "I understand your concern for the other humans. Please do not interfere with a military operation. I will return later. See to her needs," said Kai brusquely to the doctor. He turned and strode away, leaving Jenn with the medic.

Jenn lay her aching head back onto the pillow as she listened to Kai's fading footsteps.

"Where's he going?" she asked.

"I assume he intends to see the princess. You weren't the only one injured."

* * * *

Kai expected the guards at his mother's door to greet him. He did not expect them to prevent him from entering.

"I'd like to see my mother now," said Kai roughly. Typically he would have come here first, but today a force inside him wouldn't let him leave his sindare while she might be injured. After the consultation with the human doctor, Kai believed Jenn would recover. Now he wanted to find out about his mother.

After the bombs had gone off, Kai saw his mother loaded into a medical transport. The bloodied Emperor had climbed into the transport with her over the protests of his staff. Jenn was already unconscious, and Kai couldn't leave her. He had picked her up and walked through the chaotic scene, shouting orders to shell-shocked soldiers, sending them to different tasks. A medical unit had stopped Kai. When a doctor had insisted Jenn move to a medical facility, Kai left with her.

They tried to treat Kai first, but the warrior nearly snapped the doctor's head off with his screaming. He had faced many battles over the years, but it had always been his life on the line. Now the most important people in his life were injured, and he was fine. Kai was worried and frustrated. This time, he couldn't solve his problems by killing something.

The door to the suite opened from the inside. The Emperor stuck his head out the door. "Let her son come in. And as for the rest of you, get out of here." Kanton gestured to the courtiers crowded into the medical suite. They filed out one by one, some looking disheveled with ripped clothes or bloody smears on their bodies. Warrel was the last of the royal court to leave, and he gave Kai an unreadable glance.

Right now Kai couldn't care less about Warrel's jealousy. The emperor looked at Kai, his face lined with worry.

"My lord." Kai approached his mother's bed. She was stretched out on the bed and remained unconscious. She had been washed and dressed in a clean gown. He thought she would be awake.

"What's wrong?" Kai's voice sounded strained.

"She was thrown into the air by the final blast. Her head hit the ground, and she couldn't stop herself."

"Is she going to recover?"

"We don't know. The medics gave her drugs to reduce the swelling in her brain, but they've done everything they can do. Now only the gods know if she'll pull through."

"Do we know who is behind this tragedy?"

"Our intelligence suggests this is the work of a group which opposes the treaty with Earth."

Kai closed his eyes. "I will make sure I find these people and kill them," he declared.

"I have no doubt you will, but I have to tell you something. I cannot do my duty as Emperor while I help your mother recover. I have given Warrel authority until I can return. I hope you understand. Right now, Warrel is your Emperor, not me."

"My lord," said Kai. "My loyalty always goes to you."

"As a son's loyalty goes toward his father, yes," said Kanton. "That means more to me than you know. But I want to make one thing clear. Warrel deserves your loyalty as Emperor now. You must follow him."

Kai found himself unable to answer.

"And how is Jenn?"

"The humans say her injuries are not life-threatening. She will recover."

"I'm glad for you."

"My lord, maybe it would be best for the empire if I take my sindare to a place outside Anquera's influence. She is causing too many problems for you."

"Our problems started with Calan Tourab. If we had handled that situation differently, we might have better relations with Earth now."

"We've always defeated our enemies in battle!" Kai was shocked.

"Yes," said Kanton slowly. "But have we considered the costs? Is the life of your mother, my sindare, worth winning all the time? At what point does the price outweigh the benefit to the empire? If Anquera loses its princess, we will have lost our soul. Will any honor or glory be worth it?"

Kai didn't know what to say. He had never imagined he might lose his mother. But the Emperor was correct. If she went to the gods, Kanton would never recover.

"She won't leave us," assured Kai.

"Let's hope that is the case. Take your leave. I wish to be alone with her. I will send word if anything changes."

"Thank you, my lord." He put his hand on the Emperor's shoulder, an intimate gesture that tradition didn't permit in public. Kai bowed his head respectfully and left his mother with her husband watching over her.

CHAPTER 15

Jenn's head hurt. She was finding it difficult to remember what had happened to her. Jenn vaguely remembered Kai coming into her room and talking to her, but she wasn't sure what either one of them said to each other. There was a human doctor in her dreams though she wasn't sure from where.

From looking around, she thought she was in a medical facility. An Anquesh warrior was standing at attention inside her door. Jenn wondered how long he had been there. Suddenly he spoke. "My lord."

As the words came out of his mouth, the guard changed his posture, looking more formal. His appearance was slightly different from how the warriors presented themselves to Kai. Jenn heard footsteps come toward her. She tried to lift her head to see who was approaching her, but the attempted movement hurt too much. *Didn't these people know anything about pain killers?*

"Jennifer Carden," said a thin, nasal voice. An alien, one she didn't immediately recognize, walked to stand at the foot of her bed. Jenn slowly realized she had seen him before. He was standing next to the Emperor on the dais during the explosion. The alien wore his hair in smooth dreadlocks, like all the other Anquesh men she had seen, although he tied his hair into a knot on the top of his head. While he wasn't as big as Kai, he was still taller than her. He was imposing in a different way.

"We haven't been formally introduced. I am Prince Warrel, heir to the throne of Anquera."

Jenn swallowed. What was she supposed to say?

"What can I do for you?" Her words sounded sloppy and incorrect. Was she expected to say something else? Jenn dug into her brain, but the fogginess prevented her from accessing the part that held the answers.

Warrel frowned and muttered to an aide standing next to him. The unhappy look on his face caused Jenn to panic slightly. Had she just insulted a member of the royal family?

"Due to recent circumstances, my father, Emperor Kanton, has tasked me with his duties. One of the assignments is making sure the Emissary from Earth is comfortable."

Jenn studied Warrel's face. It looked smooth, like a facile representation of friendliness. But she thought his amiability was only a mask. When she looked at the alien's eyes, she saw they had a glimmer of disgust. A shiver went through her body. The Prince reminded her of a cat getting ready to pounce on a mouse.

Despite the pounding in her head, her instructions on proper protocol moved to the front of her brain and her training took over.

"That's very kind of you, your Highness." Now she was thankful for the lessons TerraMates had forced down her throat. At least she had a vague idea of how to handle

119

the creepy prince. "Commander Imwaden has been seeing to my needs until now."

"Yes," said Warrel, drawing out the word. "That may not be the case in the future."

Alarm shot through Jenn's body. What was going on? Kai had seemed insistent on staying by her side.

"Why would that be, your Highness? I thought he was the Emissary to Earth."

"Anquera needs Commander Imwaden elsewhere."

Of course. Kai didn't want her. Jenn knew this already, but she didn't understand why the Prince was making the announcement to her. He outranked Kai.

"I hope we can get to know each other better." The Prince put his hand on top of hers. "When the doctors say you are stable, you may stay at the palace as my guest."

Jenn didn't like the way Warrel looked at her. He slowly ran his eyes up and down her figure, and she thought she could see him imagining her naked body. She didn't want him to fuck her. She had the feeling his invitation had several strings attached. "That won't be necessary, your Highness."

"I assure you, it is. I would be distressed if anything else happened to you on Anquera. You are the key to the sealing the treaty with Earth. You are an honored guest, and I intend to treat you as one."

After Kai's brief tutorial about the difference between honored and hated enemies, Jenn wondered if 'honored guest' was a new status the prince conferred on her. As much as she wanted to tell the jerk to get lost, she wasn't in a position to speak her real thoughts. She had a feeling she would be more of a prisoner in the palace than in Kai's spaceship.

"I appreciate your hospitality, your Highness."

"Magnificent," said Warrel with an insincere smile. "In private, we don't need to exchange any false titles between us. You can call me lord."

"I'm overwhelmed, my lord."

Warrel nodded happily. "I'll have rooms prepared for you."

Jenn needed to speak with Kai. He may not want her, but she felt protected when she was with him. She had a feeling no one was safe with Prince Warrel.

* * * *

Kai's second-in-command, Sevit, stopped when he passed Kai. He was walking down the hall with Tal Oban, the security officer. "Commander. I didn't expect you back on the ship so soon."

He hated leaving the medical facility housing Jenn and his mother, but it seemed to Kai that no one was doing enough to address the threat. Tellen had vanished, and Warrel wasn't returning his calls.

121

"Did you inspect the Ruvien for damage?"

"Yes, sir," Sevit replied. "There is minor damage to the hull plating from the blast, but the crew is reinforcing it right now. All systems are operational."

"Good. I want all my officers in the ready room in fifteen minutes. Tal, we need all the information you have on races near our borders."

"Yes, Commander," said Tal. His face looked peculiar.

"Is this a problem?" asked Kai pointedly.

"No, sir. You're not giving me a lot of time. The files may be incomplete."

"Then get on it, Lieutenant."

"Yes, Commander."

Fifteen minutes later, his staff sat around a conference table in his office. He looked at everyone. Kai had only known them for six months. Of course, he had read their personnel files and took time to meet with them personally, but their loyalty hadn't been tested yet. Would these soldiers back him under fire? What Kai had on his mind could easily be twisted into a charge of treason.

"What do we know about these bombs?" asked Kai.

"Sir, we were prevented from further investigation by palace security. They said they would handle everything."

"Well, we started analyzing the bombs before palace security became involved. I'm sure we learned something about the instruments that attacked my family and me. Do we have any clues?"

Tal gulped. "Commander, forgive me. Palace security confiscated all the intelligence."

Kai slammed his hand on the table. "Didn't you see the information before they took it?"

"They have ordered me to keep the information secret, by Prince Warrel's command."

"Who is your commander?" Kai looked at his men, gauging their reactions.

"You are our commander," asserted Sevit. Everyone but Tal nodded their head in agreement.

"Sevit, have Lieutenant Oban escorted to the brig."

"You can't do this," protested Oban.

"Take him," said Kai dismissively. "Any warrior who shares his sentiments can join him. Warrel may be the prince, and I serve the royal family, but I am in command of my ship. Is that clear?"

"Yes, sir!" his officers responded in unison.

"Good. Let's get to work. Call up Oban's second and let's see what we can discover. We are going to find out who's behind these attacks and make them pay."

The remaining officers nodded. Sevit ordered Oban's second, Chief Nahen, to the briefing room. He was an older man. Although his dreadlocks were beginning to gray, he carried himself with a warrior's demeanor.

"Chief," said Sevit, "Do you have the records of the blast that injured the human and Princess Andeleth?"

The chief looked around the room.

"Don't bother searching for Oban," said Kai. "He declined to participate in our investigation. If you have any objections, let me know now."

"Commander, I will provide whatever you want."

"Do you have the original records of Oban's sensor sweeps?"

"No, Commander. Palace security took them all."

Kai groaned.

"I do, however, have copies."

CHAPTER 16

Kai strode through the halls of the palace, heading straight for the one place he thought held answers. He had controlled his outward appearance, but internally he felt like an animal. Kai couldn't believe Kanton had given the title of Emperor to Warrel. Up until this point, Kai had been content to let the Emperor handle the situation with Earth. He trusted his judgment.

He didn't trust Prince Warrel. In his soul, he knew Warrel was incompetent to handle the job, but he had suppressed the feeling for many years.

The security team aboard the Ruvien did a thorough examination in a short amount of time. However, all they could determine was who *didn't* send the bombs. It was important information, but incomplete. The list of suspects was slightly shorter now. Kai needed assistance figuring out the responsible part, and the person who could help him the most was imprisoned in the palace.

The last time Kai had seen him, Commodore Jeff Bretland expressed his dissatisfaction at being separated from his crew. Kai appreciated the human commander's sentiments. Any good leader would want to reunite with his people. But the Anquesh would not allow Bretland to be in a position where he could encourage his men to escape.

Until the Emperor decided the human's fate, Bretland was under house arrest.

Kai had developed a grudging respect for the human Commodore. In his mind, Bretland had moved from hated enemy to honored enemy. The Earth people may have strange ways of thinking, but some were honorable in their way, Calan Tourab aside. The Earth people had already paid for that incident. Kai wondered how much additional blood was needed to settle the debt of vengeance.

Would the Anquesh bloodlust be powerful enough to destroy both races?

A single palace guard stood at the entrance to the Commodore's suites.

"Stand aside," ordered Kai.

"The orders say he is not allowed visitors."

"This isn't a visit. It's an interrogation. I need information from the Earth man about today's attack. Are you aware the Princess was severely injured?"

"No, Commander. I mean, yes, Commander, I did hear. I'm sorry about the Princess' injuries."

"If you're sorry, follow my commands."

The man stepped aside even though he looked conflicted. Kai didn't have much time before the guard would verify if Kai had the authority to question Bretland. Kai was acting on his own. He didn't know what Warrel would do, but he suspected the Prince would not look favorably on his actions.

Bretland stood at the broad window looking out onto the city. He turned as soon as Kai entered the room.

"Commander?" said Bretland, walking toward him. He held out his hand for an Earth-style greeting. Kai shook hands vigorously, having learned this exchange from the Earth Commodore. "What is the status of my crew? I haven't heard anything about them."

"They are fine. Everyone's safely on your ships. Anquesh engineers and your crew have worked together repairing your vessels."

Bretland snorted. "You've gained knowledge about our propulsion and weapons systems at the same time, I suppose."

"Of course. As well as your holographic technology," said Kai. "But a full debriefing will have to wait for another time. Commodore, you spoke once before about a threat from one of our allies. At the time, you wouldn't tell me who they were. The political situation on Anquera has changed. Emperor Kanton has stepped down from the throne, leaving Warrel in charge."

"Good Lord," said Bretland, shaking his head.

"I share your feelings about my stepbrother. Can you tell me now? Who pretends to be our friend, but is secretly our enemy?"

"It's a race of big green aliens with bumps all over their bodies."

"The Similcue," Kai breathed. The Emperor was negotiating with them, trying to get them to help in the fight against Earth. The warrior in him was furious at the dishonorable actions of the traitorous bastards.

Before Kai could ask Bretland for more information, the broad picture window shattered with a ping, sending shards of glass flying to the ground. Instinctively Kai shoved the human to the floor, but it was too late for the Earth soldier. Blood pooled in the center of the man's chest, and pain twisted his face.

"Take care of my crew," gasped Bretland. His breathing stopped.

Kai stared at the Commodore. He had been full of life alive one minute, but an empty shell the next. He looked around the room, searching for anything that would help him understand this senseless death. In Kai's shell-shocked head, it didn't make sense to kill Bretland now. The Anquesh were taking care of the Earth crew. Who would kill Bretland and why would they do it?

Or was someone trying to kill Kai instead and missed their target?

The door opened, and a guard rushed into the room. He surveyed the scene with a flick of his eyes.

"Move away from the body, my lord."

"Get some more people in here and seal off the area. Let no one in the room other than security," Kai commanded.

"Move away, my lord, and surrender your weapons."

"What do you mean?" Kai asked warily.

"Prince Warrel ordered me to take you into custody."

"Are you daft, man? Someone murdered the Earth representative in front of my eyes."

"That may be so, but I still have my orders. It isn't obvious to me who killed Bretland. I'm just a soldier."

Within seconds, the room filled with more guards. Kai looked over all of them, silently calculating if he could subdue them all. He thought he could do it, but then what would he do? He needed ground clearance to get to his ship in orbit around Anquera, and he couldn't leave Jenn behind.

Kai decided that he was contemplating a foolish fight. More than that, he was also a person who respected the law. He would have to take his fight to another arena.

He handed his weapons over to the guard. "Take me to Warrel."

"That was my next order."

Kai looked down at the stricken man from Earth. He was a person Kai regarded in his heart as an honored enemy.

I will avenge you, Kai thought. He allowed the guards to lead him to his stepbrother.

* * * *

Kai usually took a moment to appreciate the audience hall of the Anquesh Empire. The sweeping architecture of the vast space and the glittering gathering of nobles from across the empire always gave him a sense of pride for being part of something bigger than himself.

Kai grew up at the periphery of court life. Because his mother was a commoner, she was not allowed to attend special events. One of his life's goals was to make himself the most honored of Anquera's warriors. Then his mother would have to be accepted by the court and have a presence there. Princess Andeleth didn't sit on the Queen's throne, but Kai could stand beside it and remind everyone who was the heart of Anquera.

Today Kai didn't feel like appreciating anything. The ambassador of the Similcue stood next to Warrel. Kai didn't have any proof, but he suspected Bretland knew the truth about the Similcue. Now that Bretland was dead, he could not bear witness against the dishonorable enemy. Kai didn't think Bretland's death was a coincidence. Seeing the Similcue and Anquera's leadership together made Kai's blood boil.

He didn't like that Warrel was physically sitting on the Emperor's throne. It was not improper given the circumstances, but Kai still considered it a mark of disrespect. Emperor Kanton was not dead, but Warrel already acted like he owned the office. Kai felt sick.

Instead of bringing Kai close to the throne, the guards on either side made him stop a considerable distance away. The gap was unusual and one typically given to an enemy.

So that's how it is, thought Kai.

"Commander Imwaden," said Warrel. "I am shocked."

"About what, your Highness?" Kai fought back a sneer, which he felt Warrel deserved. He would not dishonor himself or the throne by being rude to the crown prince.

"I have information that you are involved with the terrorist organization that disrupted the reception of Earth woman Jennifer Carden."

"That's ridiculous." Kai couldn't believe Warrel was attempting to sell an obvious lie.

"You've made a good show of sympathizing with the Earth people, of course. Calling Jennifer Carden your sindare. But that's a lie isn't it? You have planned to derail the marriage between you and Earth all along, making it look like they were dishonorable and broke the treaty."

"With all due respect," said Kai through gritted teeth, "I believe your Highness is misinformed."

"I don't think so, Imwaden. You were discovered hovering over the body of Commodore Bretland."

Kai stared blankly at Warrel, not believing the facts could be distorted so thoroughly.

"Arrest him," said Warrel. "I'll make sure he stands trial for his crimes. In the meantime, to keep our honor with the people of Earth, I will marry Jenn Carden."

CHAPTER 17

Jenn sat up and swung her legs over the edge of the bed. She still felt woozy, and the floor looked far away.

"What are you doing?" asked her guard.

"I need to stretch my legs. It's bad for humans to be inactive for long stretches of time."

Jenn didn't mind telling a little lie because she hated being here in the first place. It was bad enough that she was kidnapped from her planet, then tossed around like a rag doll when she first set foot on Anquesh. Now she was locked away, with a promise of future imprisonment by creepy Prince Warrel.

"Let me call the doctor," said the guard.

"Go ahead. I'm not stopping you." Jenn slid to the floor and started walking to the door.

"Wait."

"Do you think I'm going to escape? You guys are watching me every minute."

"Get a doctor to Jenn's room." She had already left the room.

She wasn't comfortable walking around in her examination gown. It was long enough to reach her knees, and shockingly thin. It seemed to have an even bigger gap in the back than hospital gowns on Earth, and she felt like everyone she saw would stare at her body. She peeked out into the corridor and checked in both directions. Seeing no one, she stepped forward even though she wasn't sure where she would go.

I should find Kai, she thought. They could help each other understand Warrel's plans. For a moment, Jenn felt lost. She was out of her league. She had trained to be a physical therapist, not fly around in spaceships, play politics, or marry big sexy aliens.

She had no clue as to what the Anquesh warrior could or would do, but she had to try to find a way out of it.

"Jenn," said her guard. "Wait."

She kept moving, and the guard followed her. In the back of her mind, Jenn remembered that Kai's mom was supposed to be in the same building. "Where is Kai's mother," she asked. But the hulking warrior looked at her with confusion. Whatever translated English to Anquesh didn't exist in the hallway.

Maybe simplifying her question would help.

"Kai."

If she focused on a single word, would it communicate her desires to the warrior?

Understanding dawned on the face of the Anquesh warrior. He made a gesture with his hand. When he walked back toward her room, she stopped and shook her head.

"Ada," she said in Anquesh, using the rudimentary language skills drilled into her by her TerraMates lessons. She crossed her arms across her chest. It meant *no* and, coupled with her body language, she hoped it would be enough to get her message across. "Kai," she said more forcibly.

The warrior grimaced but changed direction, heading to a new location. He led her down several corridors, finally ending up in front of a room with several guards in front of the entrance. He spoke with the guards posted, who shook their heads. The Emperor rushed out. He looked at Jenn and nodded his head, then raced down the hall.

A soldier escorted Jenn into the room, where she found the princess laid out on her bed. The princess was barely moving. Lights flashed above her head on an insert board. In the corner, standing so quietly that she didn't notice him at first, was a man who looked similar to the Emperor.

Still not Kai, but his mom, at least, she thought to herself. "Sorry for bothering you. I'm having some communication problems. They were supposed to take me to Kai."

"You must be Jenn. I'm Hanton, the Emperor's brother. I don't know how he's going to get through this alone."

"She's not going to make it, is she?" said Jenn.

Hanton shook his head.

"I'm sorry."

"Are you, Earthling? Or are you glad you will be a witness on the day Anquera loses its heart?"

"I am. Whatever you think of our people, most of us don't want war. But sometimes it's necessary."

"Necessary," snorted Hanton. He shook his head as he crossed his arms. "I just got married, you know."

"How would I know? We just met a minute ago."

"I think she's with child already. Now that I will be a father, I worry about the future. What kind of place will we give to our children when we fight ourselves to the brink of extinction?"

"We ask ourselves the same questions."

Hanton sighed. "Andeleth is a rare woman. She persuaded my brother. He will allow Kai to marry you."

Jenn's heart jumped. "Allow? I thought the marriage was a sure thing."

"It was not. I advised Kanton to give false support for the wedding. It was supposed to buy us time and let us negotiate with another race. Together, we would defeat you."

She swallowed hard. "You are exceptionally honest."

"It doesn't matter any longer. Kanton will not survive Andeleth's death. Whoever sent the bombs killed the Emperor as surely as if an assassin's blade found his heart. Warrel will become Emperor, and that will be the beginning of the Anquesh Empire's fall. I tried to tell Kanton, but he loves his son, and only sees the good in him. Warrel will take us to war again, with or without the Similcue's help. The battles will destroy us financially. Kai was right. The only hope for both our races is a treaty with Earth. It's unfortunate that we won't honor it."

* * * *

Kai saw red when his stepbrother announced he was going to marry Jenn. He shook as his body temperature rose and adrenaline shot through every cell of his body. The nuxmunit, the battle rage, swept over him at the thought of this dishonorable cur touching his sindare. His skin flushed with a dark blue-brown hue as his muscles bulked. He was going to kill that fucker.

"Mine!" he roared. He pushed through his guards and rushed up the dais to reach his stepbrother. Kai didn't see a person related to him on the throne. All he saw was an enemy with a frightened look on his face.

Many hands grabbed his body, preventing him from moving further. Kai thrashed and bellowed as men pulled him to the floor and held him down against his will.

"Do you see!" Warrel cried. "Kai persists in his treachery despite the presence of witnesses. Get him out of here and lock him up. When I have this business settled with Jennifer Carden, it will be time for Kai to have his trial."

Kai gave a long keening cry born of the nuxmunit, but his struggle was futile. Many warriors held him down, pushing his body and face into the unyielding stone floor.

"He's bleeding," said one fighter.

"He injured himself in a previous battle," said another. "He's torn all his stitches."

The other warriors started muttering. Kai was out of control. "Warrel, she's mine! I will kill you!"

A doctor approached Kai. "Hold him down. I need to stabilize him." He held up a large needle.

"Ouch," said one of the guards. "He's going to have a headache tomorrow."

"This way he'll have a tomorrow," said the doctor, using a little voice only Kai and the soldiers could hear. "He won't if he keeps bleeding like this."

"Get him out of here!" shouted Warrel.

The sound of Warrel's voice made Kai scream a battle cry. A sharp pain spread up his neck. He lay gasping as cold enveloped him and the nuxmunit drained from his body.

"What is going on here," shouted a loud voice from the entrance of the audience hall.

The voice registered dimly in Kai's brain as the Emperor's. The doctor instructed the warriors to turn Kai over.

A shadow stood over Kai's prostrate body. "I'm ending court," announced Emperor Kanton. "We will reconvene tomorrow!"

Kai felt sick to his stomach on the cold stone floor. He heard whispering as the massive doors to the hall closed.

"Explain yourself, son."

"Father, Kai Imwaden is a traitor!"

"That's a serious accusation. Do you have any proof? I trusted you could handle matters in my absence, but spreading false rumors is not what I had in mind."

"The Similcue ambassador gave me evidence that Commander Imwaden is a traitor."

Kai heard Kanton muttering, but the pounding in his head distracted him. His head was clearing slowly from the battle rage. The doctor's drugs were helping to drain the nuxmunit, but now he was shaking. His muscles didn't respond as he tried to pull himself off the floor.

Emperor Kanton was shouting now. "You have allowed personal feelings to get in the way of your judgment. I expected more from you, son. A good ruler must be able to put aside selfish motives for the people!"

Kai tried to reach up and get the Emperor's attention. He needed to calm down. His heart couldn't take the additional stress.

The heavy doors moved, and footsteps pounded on the floor as a messenger entered the room. "Emperor," the man said, his face drained of color. "Her royal highness..." His voice quavered and trailed off. "I'm sorry."

Kanton turned to his son, his face filled with wrath. "She needed me now, and I couldn't be with her because I was with you." The Emperor breathed in sharply and staggered as he clutched at his chest. Guards rushed to the Emperor, trying to catch him, but he slid to the floor next to Kai. His breathing was ragged. The doctor immediately turned his attention from Kai to the Emperor.

"Leave me alone," wheezed the Emperor, roughly batting the medic away. "She's gone. Nothing you do will change that." He turned to Kai and put his hand on Kai's shoulder. "I shouldn't have put you in this position. Forgive me." The emperor gasped a final time and fell silent as life left his body.

The guards in the hall started talking to each other, immediately gossiping that the Emperor recognized Kai as a son with his dying breath. Warrel stared at the two men on the floor his face twisted in rage.

"I never said I wanted to be a good ruler. My order stands," he said, looking at the guards. "Lock up Kai Imwaden. He'll stand trial after I fight Jenn Carden in the marriage ceremony."

CHAPTER 18

The next few days passed in a blur for Jenn. Once the medical staff realized she was walking around, an escort showed up to bring her to the palace. For her protection, she moved in the middle night, but the timing meant she couldn't see much of the palace. They put her in an elegant suite of rooms which she wasn't allowed to leave.

She wasn't bored for the first day. All kinds of elaborate clothing filled the closets, and it took her an entire day to go through them. In the meantime, Warrel assigned a rotating security detail to her. Jenn was thankful that they spoke some degree of English. Whatever Warrel had planned for her seemed complicated.

Kai never came to visit her, which she thought was odd. But she couldn't get any information out of her guards. Jenn felt more alone than when she was on Kai's ship. To pass the time and stretch her body, she turned to Tai Chi routines.

This morning Rotan, the head of her security detail, watched her intently as she moved from one form to another.

"What you are doing?" he asked innocently.

"It's called Tai Chi," she said. "It's a form of exercise on Earth."

"It looks like a fighting art."

"I've heard there are fighting forms, but I've never studied them."

He shook his head. "You've never looked at it the correct way before. Let me show you, with your permission."

Jenn shrugged. "Sure."

Rotan moved in front of her. "You start in a standing position."

"Right."

"Your body weight is centered. Make your next move."

Jenn went through a long-practiced routine. She turned sideways and brought her hands up, one at shoulder level, one hovering between her chest and solar plexus.

"You are still centered, but now one hand is defending your chest while the other is in a position to make an offensive move. If I move into to you, like this, what happens?"

"I scream like a girl?"

"This isn't the time for jokes, Jenn."

"Of course. I'm sorry."

"In this position, the hand at your shoulder should shoot out, cut across my chest and throw me off-center. See?"

"I've never thought about it like that."

"What's your next move?"

"I raise my leg to shift my direction."

"Where can that leg go if a man was attacking you?"

Jenn looked down. Her knee was hovering in position between the man's legs.

"Kick you in the nuts."

"Now your attacker is off-center and bent over. What do you do with your hands and arms?"

"I put my right arm out, and shift direction."

"And while you're doing that, finish the motion. Push your hand into the attackers face, pull it back, turn your body and give him nothing to hit. Tai Chi provides stability. You maintain your center of balance, preventing others from finding it and making you unstable. In return, you can redirect their moves against them."

"To me, it's just an exercise program."

Rotan shook his head. "Only a warrior race would create a fighting form and hide it in an exercise movement."

"Is that really how you think of us? Warriors?"

"Definitely. Only a few races that can stand up to the might of the Anquesh."

"Do you want to know a secret? We're stubborn."

"Whatever you want to call it, many of the warriors suspect we have met our match. It frightens the nobles."

"Kai told me that my race is considered a hated enemy."

"His statement is correct."

"Then why are you telling me these things?"

"Anquesh are allowed to think for themselves. Honor is important to us, but we show it in different ways. Emperor Warrel intends to challenge you in the wedding ceremony. He believes he will preserve the honor of the Anquesh by fulfilling the treaty with Earth."

"But Commander Imwaden..."

"That's all I can say about the matter. I encourage you to practice Tai Chi and learn to defend yourself."

* * * *

Kai was in a dark, cold cell. He had no sense of time. He knew Warrel was subjecting him to techniques designed to demoralize a prisoner. The Anquesh didn't officially sanction any form of torture, but they were all trained in the techniques. Treating a fellow warrior in this manner reaffirmed the depths of Warrel's hatred for Kai.

The Anquesh commander didn't need any torture techniques to affect him emotionally. Anquesh officers trained themselves to resist while in captivity. At worst, he was experiencing an uncomfortable inconvenience.

Kai had open, raw physical wounds, but he had practiced resisting the pain. As long as he stayed in one position, he could overcome the weaknesses of the flesh.

The thing bothering Kai was intangible. The most important people in his life were gone or out of his reach.

His mother and the Emperor were dead. Kai couldn't begin to confront the depths of his sorrow. It was a black well which threatened to suck him in. Kai had nothing to distract himself in the cell's inky darkness. He couldn't stop memories of his mother from playing over and over in his head.

Kai's father had died in battle before he could form a complete memory of him. Having a father wasn't particularly important to Kai when he was a young boy because he always had a mother. When his mother married the Emperor, Kai had a model of Anquesh male strength, even though he remained distant for political reasons.

Now they were gone.

Being separated from Jenn made him feel even worse. If he could only spend a few minutes with her, he would feel better, but right now Kai was an emotional wreck. He had a new appreciation of the bond between his mother and the Emperor.

Kai felt a consuming need to be with Jenn. It was a drive that directed each thought to her. Rather than worry about his dire situation, he wondered how Warrel was treating her. Was she in danger?

145

LISA LACE

He realized his feelings were what Anquera poets spoke of when they wrote about sindare love. If Kai ever got out of this prison, he was determined to make Warrel would pay for every death caused by the Prince's incompetence. The only thing gave him pleasure was imagining his stepbrother groveling at his feet, apologizing for every moment of Jenn's discomfort.

CHAPTER 19

When Jenn woke up, several Anquesh women hovered around her, staring down at her and smiling. She wondered how long they had been watching her sleep. One spoke to her in Anquesh and pulled insistently at the thin blanket covering her body. Jenn didn't have enough experience with the language to understand what the woman was saying to her. She looked around for help and saw Rotan standing by the door.

"Can you help me out here? Why are they looking at me?"

Rotan's face didn't show any emotion. "They are here to prepare you for your wedding fight with Prince Warrel."

"Right now? I thought someone would train me in weapons or something. What if I lose?"

"Calm down. You're going to alarm the women."

"That's ok with me. I'm plenty alarmed myself at the moment."

The woman spoke with Rotan. "Jennifer Carden, they are concerned and think they might have angered you. Please stand slowly and let them do their work. Being in the presence of a mighty Earth warrior terrifies them."

Jenn gave Rotan a sideways glance, then looked up at the alien females. They were all a head taller than her and began to wrap blankets around her as she rose from the bed.

"Why do they think I'm a fighter?"

"It's possible someone told them you had some abilities." Jenn wasn't sure, but she thought Rotan had a glint of amusement in his eye.

Jenn closed her eyes. She wasn't ready to fight someone. She would never be ready. "What do they expect?"

"After they finish with you, your security team will bring you to an arena. It's not far from here. We can escort you to the entrance, but you'll have to move to the center on your own. Prince Warrel will be waiting for you. You'll fight him until only one of you is standing. Pretty simple."

"Seems romantic. Why do the Anquesh perform this ridiculous ritual?"

Rotan blinked. "I thought it would be obvious to an intelligent Earth woman like yourself. Only a worthy warrior deserves a mate. The male has to prove he is worthy of the bride. It's her responsibility to test him in battle." The explanation sounded natural coming out of his mouth. From Jenn's perspective, Rotan could hardly understand the question.

"Why would you bother going through with this charade? Anquesh men are obviously stronger than the women."

"The battle rage makes up for deficiencies in strength. If the male is unworthy, nuxmunit will fall on the woman, and she will easily vanquish him."

Jenn looked at Rotan with disbelief in her eyes. "That sounds great if you're from Anquera. I'm from Earth. Humans don't have battle rage."

"Somehow, you'll have to find inner strength for the task ahead. I believe you are a warrior."

Jenn wasn't sure if the vote of confidence was hurting or helping her. She knew she could not prevail against the Anquesh prince.

"What happens if he wins?"

"If he wins, you'll be his wife. If you win, honor is satisfied."

"What does that mean? Honor is satisfied? Will Warrel send me home?"

One of the women started brushing her hair and made a tsking noise. That didn't need translation.

Rotan didn't answer her at first. He didn't look her in the eye, keeping his eyes averted. He seemed to be staring at the door. "It's not my place to say anything more."

Were Anquesh warriors genetically modified for stubbornness? "And what if Warrel wins?"

Rotan's eyes narrowed. "Warrel has a previous marriage contract with another royal daughter. The rumor is he intends to follow through with it."

"Sounds kinky. Do Anquesh typically take more than one wife?"

"No, Jenn, we do not."

The implications of what Rotan revealed and kept hidden were clear and chilling. Warrel had no intention of letting her live if he won the battle in the arena. If she wanted to see Kai again, she was going to have to win.

"Where is Commander Imwaden?"

The longer she was apart from Kai, the more concerned she grew about him. He talked a lot about honor, and it seemed like he took his duties seriously. She was surprised he had let her be in this situation for so long by herself.

Thinking about Kai brought a flood of memories. Being in the taxi alone together. Daily visits each day on the Ruvien during the journey to Anquesh. The feeling of tightly pressing against him when the bomb exploded, shielding her body from the worst of the blow.

Jenn was sure Kai wouldn't let harm come to her. Right?

"It's not my place to say anything more."

Jenn rolled her eyes and groaned, startling the women. Nevertheless, they began their work earnestly and after two hours of grooming, hairdressing and primping, Jess wore the wedding outfit of an Anquesh woman.

She looked at herself in a mirror. One of the women had twisted and styled her hair, shaping it into the dreadlocks and braids favored by Anquesh females. Another had trimmed and buffed Jenn's nails to a high gloss.

All of them worked together to put Jenn into an elaborate garment that featured pantaloons in a pattern of yellow, orange and brown. There were slits on the side from her upper thigh down to the ankle. They spent time adjusting a metal breastplate similar to the ones Anquesh warriors used. In the end, it was obviously too large for Jenn. Ballet-like slippers on her feet completed the ensemble.

The women bowed and murmured to themselves as they backed away and out of the room, leaving Jenn alone with Rotan.

"We should go now," said the warrior. "It is time."

Jenn trembled. Would she be able to defeat Warrel by herself?

* * * *

Jenn had a sinking feeling in her stomach when she walked into the hot, bright Anquesh sun shining into the arena. She looked around to see an enormous stadium surrounding her, filled with thousands of Anquesh. She had been nervous enough before, but now she knew there were going to be a lot of people watching the spectacle of her wedding battle.

If what Rotan said was correct, losing the fight was going to be the least of Jenn's problems. In the middle of the huge fighting area was a tent with flimsy transparent cloth covering the sides. In theory, if Warrel successfully won her, she would be having sex in that tent. From what she could tell, the fucking would be visible to the entire arena.

Hell no! There was no way she was going to perform a sex show on any planet. And she didn't want to mate with him in the first place! The thought made her insides burn. She resolved to get the best of the pompous prince somehow.

Jenn lost her confidence when Warrel stepped out of the tent. He looked more imposing than ever. Even though he wasn't as muscular as Kai, he was still than her and weighted a lot more. Jenn had one hope. The gravity on Anquesh was slightly weaker than Earth's. She thought her muscles might be equal to or even stronger than his. She had spent the past few days working on Tai Chi forms to help her control her body's response to the lighter gravity.

Warrel put his hands together and bowed his head slightly, looking up at Jenn over his hands with a fiendish gleam in his eye.

Her breastplate bothered her. It was too big and restricted her movements. She needed to get rid of it if she was going to have a chance. Jenn unlatched the breastplate, letting it fall to the ground. She shook her head, slowly moving her limbs into a Tai Chi defensive pose. A roar went up through the crowd. They wanted a good show and approved of Jenn's defiance.

The prince scoffed, and the sound reverberated around the enclosure. Apparently the acoustics in the stadium were outstanding. Jenn wondered if she could use it to her advantage. "You'll never beat me, Warrel. Are you even a match for a puny human female? You might as well give up now."

Apparently there were translators because someone repeated her comment in Anquesh over loudspeakers. Her words earned laughter and guffaws from the crowd. Warrel's face turned red.

"You need a lesson in respect," said Warrel.

Jenn stuck out her index finger and curled it toward her body, inviting Warrel to engage her.

"Bring it," she shouted. Another cheer rang around the walls.

Warrel strode toward her. Jenn carefully watched his steps. He seemed overconfident, swaggering and not bothering to defend himself.

She would show everyone he was making a big mistake by underestimating her. As Jenn patiently waited, he stepped inside her range, reaching for her shoulders. Jenn leaned back slightly then jammed the heel of her hand into the underside of his jaw, causing him to retreat. The crowded roared.

Warrel lurched forward angrily. Jenn shifted to her right foot while bringing her left knee and left hand up. Warrel found himself stumbling into her. Jenn's knee connected with his groin and her left hand struck his face. When his head snapped back, she went for his throat. He gasped and stumbled.

If she ever got back to Earth, she was going to take her Tai Chi instructor out to dinner.

The crowd got to their feet and started making loud noises, using their feet to pound on the footboards of the arena.

The follow-through from her lunge left her right leg behind Warrel's right knee. She reached under his left arm. With a quick movement, she rotated it up into a painful, off-center position. When she pushed him with her left arm, he fell to the ground.

If she had thought the crowd was wild before, getting Warrel off his feet sent them into a new frenzy. Someone started chanting her name, and the group picked it up. The arena rumbled as the aliens cried out, "Jenn! Jenn!"

She had never seen such a look of hate like the one she saw on Warrel's face. He sat on the ground studying her, scrubbing his jaw and rubbing his throat with his hands.

"I will kill you," he murmured.

No one heard his threat over the roar of the crowd. Jenn was surprised he had the balls to challenge her again. "Not today." She kicked him as hard as she could in the groin. When he started howling in pain, she turned and headed toward the exit of the arena. She ran as fast as her slippered feet would carry her.

As she tried to escape, the first bolts of intensely bright light scored the floor of the arena. People began to scream and scrambled for the exits.

* * * *

When the cell door opened, Kai thought his luck might finally be turning. He moved into a relaxed position to camouflage his true intentions. He formed his hands into fists at his sides and waited for a chance to escape.

The light spilling in from the hallway blinded him. It took a moment for his eyes to adjust to the faint light.

"Is he in there?"

"Commander." Kai recognized the voice. It was Sevit, his second-in-command. "Are you able to stand and walk?"

"Sevit! I never thought I'd be this glad to see you."

"We've all been worried about you since your arrest."

"Well, I'm still alive. But why are you here? I've haven't seen a soul since they locked the doors on me. I thought I might rot in here."

"I don't believe you have to worry about that. Prince Warrel hasn't forgotten about you. In fact, he's announced a public trial for your crimes. Once they find you guilty, you'll be executed."

"It's good to know I'll be getting a fair trial, at least."

155

"This is not the time for jokes. We've done the orbital sensor sweeps you requested, and we have a problem. There's a large fleet at the edge of our solar system. It would only take one quick jump to bring them within the range of Anquera. I tried to inform central command, but no one will take my calls."

"Do you have a plan?"

"I've contacted many of the fleet commanders. The good news is half of them are ready to follow you into battle. The bad news is the others have reported me for treason. We've hidden the Ruvien behind one of the fourth planet's moons. I have a shuttle tucked away in the northern palace gardens for our escape."

"You know they can execute both of us at the same time, right? They don't have to wait for your trial."

"I cannot allow the destruction of Anquera. If they call me a traitor, so be it. I know I will have fulfilled my duty as a protector of the empire."

Kai grabbed Sevit's shoulder. "We'll need warriors like you in the upcoming battles. What about Jenn?"

"The Earth woman? She's in trouble. At this very moment, Prince Warrel is performing the marriage ceremony with her."

"Already? That's impossible. How can she stand a chance against a fully-trained warrior?"

One of Sevit's men was loitering in the background, listening to something on his communicator. "She did it!" he exclaimed.

Sevit frowned. "I thought I told you to turn your transmitter off the battle and stay focused on our secure channel."

"Yes, sir. I'm sorry, but I put down a few credits on the human. It sounds like Jenn landed the first blow. She scored a direct hit on his cock. He's going to have problems using it tonight."

"I've got to get to her," said Kai.

"We're using the marriage ceremony as a cover for our activities. It's the only way we were able to penetrate the defenses. If we stop to retrieve Jenn, I can't guarantee our escape."

"If I escape and leave her by herself, it's pointless. She is my sindare. I have to get her."

Sevit shook his head.

"By the gods!" exclaimed the gambler.

Sevit shot him a severe glance.

"Sorry, my lord. Jenn just upended the Prince, but he's angry now, and she's frightened. I'm going to double my money."

"Jenn!" said Kai in a strangled voice.

157

"If we need to get her, then we need to get her. The way out of the palace is clear. Everyone is watching the fight. I'll get the shuttle as close to the arena as possible. Take my transmitter." Sevit pulled out his earpiece and passed it to Kai. "We can't locate you without it."

Kai clasped Sevit's shoulder. "Thank you," he said.

"I think this is the first time a bride has tried to run out of the arena!"

"Go, Commander!" said Sevit. "May the gods run with you!"

Kai took off, running for Jenn's life, racing through corridors of the palace he knew like the back of his hand. He moved out into the gardens and toward the gates that would take him to the city streets. The arena only a few blocks away. It wasn't far by any rational measure, but to Kai, at that minute, it seemed a universe away. He felt his heart hammering against his chest.

He knew Warrel was a miserable bastard and would drag Jenn back into the arena so he could finish the fight. Kai was proud that Jenn seemed to be holding her own, but there was no telling when the nuxmunit would come upon the Prince. Warrel would not want to be humiliated by a human in front of his people.

While Kai was thinking, he saw the telltale flashes of laser cannons firing into the arena. He didn't think he could move any faster, but somehow he sped up.

Hang on, Jenn. He wished he could telepathically communicate his thoughts to her. *I'm coming for you as fast as I can.*

CHAPTER 20

Jenn's heart hammered against her chest as her feet flew over the ground. The crowd was trying to disperse but couldn't get out of the way fast enough. Spectators screamed in fear from the stands as streaks of white fire strafed the arena floor.

The few remaining security guards tried to steer people out of the stands and keep them from panicking. Jenn looked over her shoulder to see Warrel running away from her. A group of Anquesh soldiers formed a protective ring around him as he exited.

He left the arena while she was still inside.

I beat him.

Jenn didn't have time to savor her victory before a loud crack split the air in half, followed by a boom. Jenn stumbled on the ground. It started vibrating and soon the entire stadium was shaking. More screams rose from the chaos of the audience, who began to renew their efforts to get out of the arena.

They were going to turn into a mob soon. The writhing mass of bodies was about to become a stampede in the levels above her.

Jenn regained her footing and sprinted to the arch that marked her entrance to the stadium floor. She didn't know where to go, but she had to get out of the doomed structure. Before passing through the arch, a shadow stretched over her body. She looked up. Large ships hovered above the city. Streaks of laser fire were

160

everywhere, and Jenn realized there might not be a good place to hide.

The overriding instinct to survive drove her forward. She thought she might be able to find a place to wait out the attack. If she survived the destruction, the ensuing chaos might allow her to connect with Bretland and his crew. She could get a ride back to Earth.

It was a faint hope, but it was as good as she was going to get. She knew one thing for sure. She had enough of the Anquesh, their warriors, and their stupid ideas of what it took to settle a treaty.

Beyond the arch was a flood of Anquesh bodies. These were the ones who had successfully made it out of the stands. They came down from stairs that serviced the stadium's spectator levels. Jenn knew she would stand out in the crowd - she was a short blonde woman in a world of tall brunettes.

A discarded scarf lay on the ground. It was a little dirty, but it was all she had. She picked it up and wrapped it around her head, making sure to tuck all of her hair under the fabric. With luck, she would be able to pass for a younger alien and blend in among the other people trying to escape.

During the fight with Warrel, she realized she had been right about the effect of Earth's gravity on her body. Even without the nuxmunit, she was a little faster and a little stronger than an Anquera native. Her Earth strength helped her hold her own against the mass of people pressing around her, moving without direction as the ground rocked and shook under them.

161

Eventually, her group spilled into the streets. The exterior of the stadium was less crowded but still clogged with fleeing Anquesh. Jenn pressed herself against the enormous stadium wall and surveyed the tumultuous scene. Most people were running to the left. Jenn wondered if they were fleeing to safety or away from danger. A small fighter flew down the road, firing laser blasts at the aliens on the street.

Anquesh screamed and wailed as bodies fell to the ground. Another flash of white light temporarily blinded Jenn. When her vision came back, the building on the opposite side of the street was engulfed in flames. Fire and sparks erupted from the site, and the building gave a final roar as it crashed to the ground, filling the air with debris and smoke.

Jenn started coughing. She decided to move to the right, against the crowd, in the opposite direction of the oncoming aircraft. She was afraid more ships would come firing their weapons. Jenn stayed close to the buildings, hoping they would protect her from any stray laser blasts, and not be the victims of more explosions.

She passed people on the street who were moaning and gasping. She wanted to stop at each one and see if she could do anything to help them, but physical therapy was not the same thing as emergency medicine, and she knew nothing about alien anatomy. Jenn tried to avoid eye contact with the injured people and pushed forward. She walked by Anquesh of all types and ages - children, mothers and fathers. Whoever had decided to attack was cruel and cold-hearted. It was one thing to fight a battle against trained warriors, but quite another to bring a war to the general population.

She wondered if Earth was behind the attack.

Jenn passed a side street on her right. She saw something running down the street toward her. With a shock, she realized it wasn't another random Anquesh warrior. It was Kai, and he was screaming her name.

She was happy to see him but didn't want them both to die. He was next to her in a second. He didn't speak a word, but picked her up and tossed her over his shoulder.

She pounded on his back with her fists. "I can move by myself!" she shouted.

Kai barely paid attention to her and sprinted back down the street. He ran much faster than Jenn thought possible, considering he was carrying a one hundred and fifty-pound woman. Jenn bounced around on his back as he held her legs.

He began shouting something in Anquesh. Jenn had no idea what he was saying. For all she knew, he could be swearing at her because she weighed too much. Well, she never was good at dieting, though now it seemed like maybe she should have put more effort into it.

Things around them started exploding. Kai spoke into his communicator. A large shadow passed over their bodies. When Jenn looked up, a small spaceship hovered overhead. A hatch opened in the metal underbelly of the ship, and a ladder descended in front of them.

"Hold on, sindare," yelled Kai. He shifted her to his

back. "Grab my neck tightly." With a frightening growl, she felt his muscles contract beneath his body. He leaped from the ground, grabbing the bottom rung. Kai climbed it rapidly like a predator sprinting after its dinner. Jenn's breath caught in her throat when she looked down. The ground was slipping farther and farther away.

When he reached the opening, many hands reached out to haul them into the spacecraft. A pair of hands peeled Jenn away from Kai. He made a frightening growl as the hatch beneath them closed. His face contorted in anger, his eyes were wild, and his muscles flexed like he was about to attack.

A voice crooned out from the shadows behind Kai in a calming tone. The warrior holding Jenn backed away from her. Jenn was left to face Kai and his battle rage by herself. He looked like he could kill something. Kai took a step forward, and Jenn shrieked, convinced that the alien had only retrieved her to hurt her. Perhaps he blamed her for the attack on his people. Nothing the Anquesh did made sense to Jenn.

When Kai saw the fear in her face, he retreated. His twisted face looked hurt and confused. Behind him, Jenn could see the Anquesh warrior who was trying to calm him down with his voice. Jenn didn't understand all the words, but she thought he spoke Kai's name several times.

Kai let out a roar that made the room shake. The other man gave a cry for help and other Anquesh started filling the room. One of them held a syringe. As Anquesh warriors restrained Kai, he plunged the needed into Kai's neck. He was struggling against the soldiers until the end.

Jenn watched the scene in horror. She couldn't believe she had witnessed Kai's metamorphosis into the unreasoning beast in front of her. She watched the injection take effect. He slowly sank to the floor of the ship, panting, sweaty and spent.

Once Kai had calmed down, some of the Anquesh warriors helped Kai get back on his feet. They guided him toward Jenn, but she was still terrified. She looked around for a place to hide.

The ship started to vibrate, and the warriors began shouting. The men began to rush Kai out of the room, but not before he turned his eyes to Jenn. He spoke one sentence in English before they took him away. "I know you are my sindare."

The Anquesh warrior who tried to calm Kai walked toward Jenn. "You haven't seen an Anquesh warrior in the nuxmunit before, have you?

"He was like that once before during an attack on Earth. It made him stronger, but not crazy. This time, he looked out of control."

"The commander has entered nuxmunit too often in a short amount of time. It takes a toll on the body. Each time he responds to a threat, it increases the reaction. We have given him medicine to sedate him."

The floor moved violently again. "We're running out of time. Come with me. The commander needs you now."

"Why would he need me?"

"You just won your wedding battle." It was a statement, not a question, but Jenn didn't understand what he was saying.

"Of course I did. That motherfucker ran off with his tail between his legs."

"Prince Warrel has tried to influence public opinion and paint a picture of Commander Imwaden as a man without honor. He tried to steal you from the Commander under the pretense of fulfilling our agreement with Earth. You were willing to fight Warrel and defeat him in battle. It was more than a wedding ceremony. You sent a message to Anquera. People think you are fighting for the honor of Kai Imwaden."

"Look, I was trying to stay alive, and not get raped in front of a crowd."

"Your intentions don't matter, Jennifer. How your actions are perceived is important. Right now, you are important to the Anquesh. I'll be honest with you. Kai is the only remaining member of the royal family capable of leading us to victory against our enemies. Right now, we need you to stand with him in front of the soldiers. Show us you believe in the Earth agreement. You can help us out of our mess."

CHAPTER 21

"Back off, lieutenant," said Sevit. "You can see nuxmunit has immersed the Commander. Stay away from the Earth woman. He thinks she's his sindare. Move away so he sees you aren't a threat."

Even though the alien walked away from Jenn, Kai only growled some more.

Mine! was the only thought he had in his head. Kai wanted to tear the warrior apart for touching his sindare. He moved to retrieve her, but she started to scream. Her face was lined with fear, not showing the smooth loving features of a sindare proud to have her mate fighting for her.

Did she want that other male? He could easily fix that problem. Kai roared a challenge to the warrior. He would fight his rival to the death.

"Doctor, he's not calming down!" called Sevit. "Everyone help me restrain the commander!"

Bodies rushed at Kai, blocking him from reaching his mate. He struggled until he felt a sharp pain jab him in the neck. Immediately he felt dizzy and lightheaded. The strength drained from his body and slowly reason returned to his mind.

Kai rose shakily to his feet.

"Take him to the bridge," called Sevit.

As they passed by Jenn, he couldn't resist saying something to her. "Sindare?" he called gently. It felt terrible to see the fright in her eyes. Did she realize he was prepared to fight for her? Or was she merely frightened of him? He didn't have the opportunity to say anything else. His warriors led him out of the loading hatch and through the short corridors of the transport. The ship was violently rocking the entire time.

"Are we under attack?" said Kai.

"Yes, commander," said one of the warriors. "We're only on a transport ship, but we've upgraded the shields from what we've learned of Earth technology."

"Let's hope they hold up." The shields of the Earth ships had impressed the Anquesh. They were more efficient and seemed to take more hits before failing. He waved the warriors away. "I can walk by myself."

"Of course you can, commander." They released him but hovered around in case he lost control of himself again. Kai's head hurt from the shock of entering and exiting the battle rage. He had now an injection to reduce nuxmunit twice within seven days, which wasn't healthy. But he was determined his men would not see him in a weakened state.

Kai walked onto the bridge of the transport. The officer sitting in the captain's chair stood and saluted. "Commander, we are entering the upper atmosphere of Anquera. We're almost out of her gravity well."

"Is anyone pursuing us yet?"

The officer smiled. "No, Commander. Apparently the Earth shield upgrades have the side effect of concealing our movement."

"But they were firing at us."

"They were aiming at our projected flight path, nothing more. When we changed our course, we were able to avoid additional damage.

No wonder it seemed like the Earth ships could suddenly appear in battle, thought Kai. It made sense. Any technology capable of producing phantom ships might be able to cloak as well. Perhaps an alliance with Earth people wouldn't be as distasteful as it seemed if it could provide technology like this to Anquera.

"Unfortunately, the Ruvien is in orbit and not faring as well. A squad of Similcue ships is attacking."

Sevit entered the bridge with Jenn. He bent over and whispered in her ear. She nodded her head and slowly walked to Kai.

"Commander," she said. He noticed her Earth words came out in Anquesh. Sevit had activated the ship's translation protocols so Jenn would understand the conversations around her. Kai saw fear in her eyes. Did she want to be somewhere else? For the first time, he thought she might only be here for the treaty, and she was merely playing a role for her government.

"It's good to see you, Jenn." Kai settled back in the command chair. "Are there any problems with our approach to the Ruvien?"

"The Ruvien has her shields up. The Similcue ships are beginning their attack."

Kai watched helplessly as the Ruvien took multiple rounds of fire from the assault squadron. Their transport had no weapons and couldn't participate in the fight. He calculated how long it would take before the Similcue ships disabled the Ruvien's shields. The Similcue would break through the Ruvien's defenses in a few minutes. His fist curled on the armrest of his chair.

"She can't take much more of this. After the Ruvien goes, we're next."

"Sir!" said the communications officer. "The Ruvien is receiving an encrypted message. Some spaceships from Earth are going to assist us. They say the calvary is coming."

"What does that mean?"

Kai felt something brush his fist, and he saw Jenn's hand touch his.

"It's an Earth expression."

On the screen showing their surroundings, five Earth ships shimmered into existence behind the Similcue spacecraft, immediately launching volleys of laser fire.

The Similcue ships exploded one after another, disintegrating into a large debris field.

The bridge crew cheered.

"We're not done yet. We have to dock with the Ruvien. Send a message that we will be boarding."

"Yes, sir. The computer has calculated the approach vector. We'll need to drop our shields so the Ruvien's computer can detect our ship and pull us in."

"Proceed," said Kai.

"A single Similcue fighter is on our tail," said the communications officer. "Their weapons are locked onto our ship. They're too close to us. The Earth ships won't be able to attack it without risking our ship in the process."

On the bridge, screens showed multiple views of the Ruvien and the transport's surroundings. Most of the display was empty, but a movement caught Kai's eye. It showed a combat ship moving directly to their location.

Jenn saw it too. "Can we shoot it down?" she whispered.

Kai looked at his sindare's fear-filled face. "We're on a transport vessel. We don't have any weapons." He turned to the navigator. "Hard to starboard."

As the ship maneuvered to the right, a lance of laser fire barely missed their wing.

"They're charging their weapons again, sir."

The ship was getting close to the Ruvien now, and there wasn't much space to maneuver. "Tell the Ruvien to open the landing bay. We're going to have to do a hot landing."

"Sir? I'm not sure I can do it manually."

"Ensign, if you don't, we're all going to die anyway."

"Yes, my lord," said the navigator.

"Jenn, find a chair and strap in."

She looked around nervously. Spying an unoccupied seat, Jenn moved toward it and started to fasten the belts that would secure her to the seat.

"We're receiving a communication from the Ruvien." The view on the central screen changed to the command deck of Kai's ship.

"Transport, you can't land like this. In the best-case scenario, you're going to blow yourselves up. In the worst-case scenario, you're going to destroy both ships."

"Lieutenant," said Kai. "Clear the deck for us. We don't have a lot of options." The screen went blank as the transport shuddered.

"We were hit on the port side engines, sir."

"We're not going to last out her much longer. Take us to the Ruvien."

The spaceship lurched toward the underbelly of the Ruvien. A hole opened in the sleek plating of the larger spacecraft, inviting them to safety. The small vessel shook once more when it was struck by enemy fire again.

"Commander, another fighter is approaching our position." Kai cursed. "I don't think we can take another hit."

The new combatant moved faster than the Similcue fighter, closing the distance between the two, but Kai noticed that the profile was different. He wondered if the Similcue had a new experimental craft. Laser fire erupted from the new ship, and Kai braced himself for impact.

Instead of hitting the transport, the laser blasts slammed into the Similcue fighter, which broke apart in a silent explosion of light.

"We're being hailed." The forward screen flickered, revealing a human staring at them.

"There's more of them coming. If you plan to dock with your bigger ship, I suggest you do it now."

The screen flickered again, and the human disappeared. Kai made a mental note to find out how the humans had broken Anquera's communication security. The humans had more tricks up their sleeves than magicians.

Jenn sat quietly in her chair with a grim expression on her face. She was tightly clutching the edge of the armrest with her fingers. They had turned white. Kai tried to give her a reassuring smile, but she turned away when she looked at him.

He shook his head. When the battle was over, he didn't know how he was going to win the heart of his sindare.

The open bay door was approaching quickly. The navigator's hands shook as his fingers danced over the control panel. Docking was usually an automatic process, but it was slow, and they needed every second. The ensign had reduced the transport's speed, but they were still coming in too fast for a smooth landing.

The Ruvien's body Ruvien enveloped them, and suddenly they were in the landing bay. The navigator activated braking jets to slow their crash into the deck. The ship began skidding down the deck, rushing toward a bulkhead at the far end of the bay. Kai held his breath as flames engulfed the transport; the jets were now in an oxygenated environment. With a final lurch, the vessel stopped when it crashed into a wall.

Kai gathered himself, stood up, and helped Jenn to her feet. "Let's go to battle stations."

CHAPTER 22

Anquesh warriors escorted Jenn into the larger ship. Kai turned and held out his hand toward her, and immediately the soldiers pulled away to give her space so she could reach the commander. Reluctantly she took his hand. It was so large that its palm engulfed hers. He walked forward confidently while different officers gave him status updates.

He spoke curtly to the men surrounding him, and they all moved off, leaving Jenn and Kai alone in the corridor.

"I need to talk to you about something," he said, staring into her eyes. "The commander of the Earth ships has contacted us. He wants to know two things. First, he is asking about their leader, Commodore Bretland. Second, they wonder if we are going to let them leave Anquesh space. I know this might be difficult for you, but right now I need every bit of leverage I can get. Will you help me on the bridge and explain to them about the treaty between Earth and Anquera?"

"Isn't the deal contingent on us getting married?" said Jenn bitterly.

"My government is in chaos right now. Half the fleet has rallied under me, which is something I didn't intend. The lack of confidence in my stepbrother's ability to rule has created a division. I have no idea if the treaty will remain valid in the coming days. The best choice is to assume it's valid. I need every ship I can get. If that means relying on Earth ships, so be it."

Jenn felt uneasy. She was being asked to take

responsibility for her race again.

"What happens if I don't?"

"The Similcue will win, and make us their prisoners.
They'll shoot me on sight. I don't know what will
happen to you precisely, but they aren't known for being
kind to their captives."

"I guess I don't have much choice. Anything else I
should know?"

"Someone has to tell them that Commodore Bretland is
dead."

She sagged against Kai for a moment, then pulled herself
together. "I can't believe it. I only found out he was
alive a little while ago. Did the Anquesh finally kill him?"

"I was in the room when it happened. An assassin
murdered him. It wasn't us. I suspect the Similcue are
responsible."

"Do you have any proof?"

Kai sighed. "I don't have any evidence, only a hunch.
The timing of the death is suspicious. It certainly helped
the Similcue's plans."

"I think I'm going to need something more definite than
that. I'm not going to tell the United Earth Alliance
something questionable to manipulate them into assisting
their enemies. Is this the Anquesh concept of honor?
Lying to get what you want?"

"We're facing a life-and-death situation, Jenn."

"There's a saying on Earth. The ends don't justify the means. Do you only pay attention to your honor when it is convenient to you?"

"Of course not. There's no need to be offensive."

"It seems like it to me. From my perspective, honor was a convenient excuse to judge and wage war on an entire species for the actions of a few that offended you."

The expression on his face changed, twisting into a look of pain, as if she had hit him with a brick.

"Neither of our species will be around to have this argument if we don't figure out what to do," he said grimly.

Jenn stared thoughtfully at the hulking Anquesh warrior and realized he was right. If she didn't follow through with Kai's plan, both of their species were doomed.

"This discussion isn't over," she snapped. "But to buy us some time to continue it, I'll do what you want."

Kai opened his mouth in preparation to argue, then stopped when he realized she had acquiesced. His eyes crinkled with amusement as he gazed at her. In a swift motion, he swept her into his arms as if she was weightless, and crushed his lips against hers. As his warm mouth tenderly touched her, Jenn realized that in front of her was the sexy alien haunting her dreams. She melted into him, drawn to the strength of his body. Heat and tingles of energy ignited in her core. She sought more of those feelings as she clung to Kai and pressed her body against him.

She heard a voice from far away. "Commander."

Kai pulled away. "Yes, Sevit."

"The Earth captain is waiting to speak with you."

Kai bent his head slightly and closed his eyes with a sigh. "Sorry," he whispered. "I couldn't help myself." He turned quickly to Sevit while clasping Jenn's hand. "Let's go talk to him, then."

Kai held her hand all the way to the bridge, his heart still pounding of from the memory of that single stolen kiss. Being with his sindare was just like stories told to him as a child. He could barely control himself when he was around her. To Kai, Jenn had never looked more beautiful. He was attracted to her defiance. Her eyes held a challenge that was irresistible to Kai's soul.

He carefully inspected her face to see if the kiss had any effect on her, but he couldn't read her inscrutable expression. She seemed focused on moving forward and looking at the path in front of her. By the gods, he loved that aspect of her. At that moment, he realized that he had not found an Anquesh love because the women of his species didn't have what he needed. He had never refused a challenge in his life, but the women on Anquera who found him attractive seemed all too eager to please and too easy for him to take. There was no challenge, and that did not ignite a fire in his heart.

The woman next to him, the one whose hand he was holding? She was all challenge. He would have to find a way into her wayward human heart and forge a bond with her so she could feel the same sensations. Kai knew he wouldn't have the natural connection with Jenn that Anquesh sindares felt for each other. It was new territory. Learning how to love the human and the adventure of overcoming her resistance excited him.

He should have realized he had fallen for her when they first met. Kai wasn't merely a sindare with a chemical need for his mate, but an alien who found the one woman who captured his heart.

They followed Sevit onto the bridge. The vast expanse of the Ruvien's command deck spread in front of them. In a half-circle, Anquesh soldiers manned gleaming workstations stations. A multi-part viewing screen flashed different images of the area around the ship.

"Officer on the deck." The bridge crew stood.

"At ease. Turn on the translator so we can all hear the news from Earth. Bring the communication onscreen." Kai wanted to make sure his crew could understand Jenn's words. Some of his senior staff came from influential noble families in the empire. They would speak with the relatives about the decisions made on the Ruvien.

The screen shimmered and filled with the image of a human. He stood on the deck of his ship, staring into the bridge of the Ruvien. Beside him lurked an Anquesh lieutenant.

"Report," snapped Kai.

"Earth captain Ron Oakland offers his ships in defense of Anquera, Commander. He is concerned about the fate

179

of Commodore Bretland."

And now we have to tell him the Commodore is dead. Kai looked to Jenn helplessly, and she stepped forward.

"Captain, I'm Jennifer Carden. Earth sent me to Anquera with orders to help facilitate a treaty with the Anquesh."

"I hadn't heard of that project. Are you an ambassador?" said the captain. "Where were you stationed before your engagement on Anquera?"

"Not exactly. It's complicated. Who I am is irrelevant, but I do have some information for you. I'm sorry to be the one to inform you that someone assassinated Commodore Bretland."

"Was it these Anquesh bastards?"

"At this time, we don't know who did it."

"Jenn," hissed Kai quietly. She waved her hand at him.

"But they strongly suspect the Similcue was behind the Commodore's death, the same race that is attacking them now. The Anquesh commander, Kai Imwaden, the alien next to me, is trying to form a unit of mixed forces to fight against the Similcue. Will you help us?"

Oakland looked away a second then turned his eyes back to Jenn. "Of course we will help. Bretland was a good man. He didn't deserve to die in this God-forsaken place."

Kai didn't react to the insult. He couldn't afford to demand his honor at this moment. Perhaps Jenn was right. Anquera emphasized honor at convenient times. He needed the assistance of Earth.

"All of Anquera thanks you," said Kai. "We will relay instructions to you through our tactical console." The screen shimmered, and a view of the planet replaced it. Similcue ships surrounded the world. "Sevit, get in touch with all the Anquesh ships you can find and discover if they're ready for battle."

"Yes, sir."

He looked at Jenn in wonder. "Did you know he'd agree even though we didn't have proof it was the Similcue?"

"I had a hunch," said Jenn with a grin. "We're not the most advanced species in the universe, but we know how to put two and two together."

CHAPTER 23

Kai entered into commander mode as reports bombarded him from all sides. Jenn watched as he nodded his head and gave a few orders, then walked to a pedestal. He waved his hand over it, making the pedestal shimmer and display a planet with different ships hovering around it. Other soldiers gathered around him. Forgotten, Jenn found a seat and listened.

"The faint green dots represent disabled Similcue vessels. The functional ones have gone into hiding on the dark side of the third moon, Commander," Sevit said.

"What about these ships in red?" Jenn motioned with her hand. "Are they the earth spaceships? Why are there only seven of them?"

"Three of their ships were severely disabled in the fight. Our mechanics cannibalized them. We used their parts to repair the others, making a total of seven functional ships.

Kai shook his head. "Seventeen against twenty. The odds are not in our favor."

Sevit finished explaining the diagram. "The blue dots are Anquesh ships which have engaged the enemy in battle while the white wait near the fourth planet."

"Are they responding to hails?"

"No, sir."

"What do we know about Similcue invasion tactics?"

"They typically soften up a planet with direct attacks on public areas. They follow up by eliminating defenses from orbit, then regroup and attack remaining defensive forces. The Similcue don't strike first. They'll wait for us to position our ships and show our defensive strategy, then choose our weakest point to destroy us. They're probably using the downtime to analyze our possible responses and develop plans to counter them all."

"Thank you for the analysis. If it's correct, we have a big job ahead of us. Gentlemen, I want your recommendations in fifteen minutes. Inform the Earth commander that I wish to speak to him. When he's available, direct the call to my ready room."

Kai turned to Jenn. "Come with me." He held out his hand as if he expected her to take it. She looked nervously around the room and saw no one was paying any attention to the insignificant human. Biting her lip, she stood and walked to the Anquesh warrior, who smiled.

He led her to an office adjacent to the bridge. It was a small room, filled with trophies behind glass cases and a large map of solar systems laid out in star clusters. When Kai closed the door shut behind them, they were alone.

"Why are we here?" Jenn asked.

"Two things." Kai moved closer to her. "First, I wanted a couple of minutes alone with you."

183

"Well, that's thoughtful, I suppose."

"Second, I want you to speak to Oakland and ask him for a favor."

"You want an awful lot from me." Jenn pushed Kai away and folded her arms.

"I do," Kai agreed. He moved back and put his arms around her waist. "I realized something today."

"What did you understand?" she asked, licking her lips. For some reason, they suddenly felt dry.

"I know why I want you."

Jenn shook her head. Even though she couldn't believe what she was hearing, she knew something was different when he lowered his head and lightly kissed her neck under her ear.

"Let me explain something to you. Legends say that when we meet our sindare, we cannot help but feel an overwhelming desire for them. Our scientists say it is a chemical compulsion. Apparently it's a way to ensuring our species will survive. Our concerns are war, battle, and competition. It's unusual for us to pay attention to the future unless we cross paths with our sindare."

She was at a loss for words but gasped when he licked behind her ear.

"Have I mentioned that you are delicious?"

Jenn put her hands to his chest in a half-hearted attempt to push him away. For some reason, she couldn't find the strength to follow through. "I don't recall you saying anything of the sort."

"Do you see? I have been remiss with my attentions. Please forgive me."

"Perhaps I would if I understood more about this conversation."

"I worried I had offended you after our time in the taxi. You remember that, don't you?"

He began fondling her breast with his hand, drawing his thumb over the peak. Her nub hardened and sharpened her sensations. The tingles spread from her breast down to between her legs.

"How could I forget?"

"I had questions. Had I had inadvertently repulsed you? Perhaps I violated an important human custom. We are aliens to each other, and we do things differently." His hand was under the fabric now. The feeling of his fingers was electric against her flesh. He gently pinched her nipple.

"Some things are the same everywhere in the universe. Aren't you worried about violating me now?"

"I think my problem is that I like to worry." He leaned in hungrily, pressed his lips against her mouth, searching for something. As he leaned against her, she felt his hard

185

cock press into her stomach. "Nothing has come easily to me. I enjoy love competition more than most Anquesh."

Jenn looked up and over Kai's shoulder. The wall was full of trophies which extended to the ceiling. "I can see that."

"I believe you are my greatest challenge, Earth woman."

"Are you sure? Your biggest conquest over two planets?"

"Definitely," he breathed into her ear. He trailed his tongue sensuously in and around her earlobes. No one had ever done that to her before, and she felt something shift in her sex.

"Maybe we aren't different after all," she panted.

"I think it's time to find out."

"I thought we were supposed to do things first. The marriage ceremony? A battle..." Words failed Jenn as Kai slipped his fingers through the slits in the cloth on her thighs and up to her core, searching for the source of her heat.

"We had our moment of battle in the closet when we met. You won. My heart is your prisoner."

Fuck, she thought. *He even talks a good game.*

"It's my turn to win you," he said as his finger found her folds.

Jenn groaned as he touched her entrance and teased it with his fingers. They were big, but he moved them carefully. He pulled at the fastening of her pants, finding a button that magically released the flimsy fabric, leaving it around her ankles.

"So hot and wet," he murmured, his eyes half-open. Kai lifted her body and spread her legs on a chair in front of his desk. He dropped to his knees and threw her feet over her shoulders.

He put his fingers on either side of her entrance. "It's beautiful. You're like a delicate pink flower." He lowered his head and ran his tongue over her pussy, making Jenn shiver.

"The taste is fantastic." He buried his face between her legs again, moving his tongue everywhere. Where he found her clit, she gasped, and her moaning encouraged him to do more. He licked and sucked enthusiastically as her moans grew sharper and louder. Jenn clutched at his hair, pulling him deeper between her legs. She exploded with waves of pleasure that drove all thoughts from her mind.

Jenn's hips pushed against his face as he drove his tongue inside her, starting another burst of pleasure. "Oh my God."

Kai raised his head and gave her a wicked smile. "Did I win you, Jenn?"

"We can give you the round, but the fight isn't over yet."

"Good," he said with a broad grin. "I like a challenge."

CHAPTER 24

A sharp buzz rang through the little room. It sounded like a doorbell.

"Duty calls," Kai said. He pulled away and Jenn felt a pang of disappointment. She wanted to do a lot more with this passionate alien even though time and circumstances were conspiring against them. He rose, gently pulling Jenn up with him.

"I'm still shaking. It might take me a while to put my clothes back on." She looked down at her nude lower body. She felt her face growing hot with embarrassment.

"Sit behind my desk. Only you and I will know what you're wearing."

He tossed her pants at her as she scrambled to sit on his big chair. She quickly covered her lap.

Kai wiped his face with his arm, giving her a broad grin. "Maybe you should leave them off. I can't wait for round two."

"Oh my God," breathed Jenn. Secretly, she admitted that she liked the idea.

"Enter," said Kai, sinking into the chair Jenn had occupied only minutes before. He looked casual and confident. Jenn wished she could fake half of his bravado.

A soldier entered the room. "Commander, Oakland has docked with our ship and wanted to speak with you himself. He's waiting outside your quarters.

Oh no! thought Jenn. *Please don't let him in here right now. Let me put on these pants, at least.*

"Tell him to enter. I have no secrets."

Fuck! Jenn started to panic. She didn't have time to put on her clothes, but she tried unsuccessfully to move her chair closer to the desk.

Oakland entered wearing blue coveralls decorated with the patches of the United Earth Alliance. He glared at Kai. "Is it true?" he asked, with an element of challenge in his voice.

Kai looked up the captain. "Is what true?" he said evenly.

"Has Earth sold this woman to you?"

"What do you mean? No trading took place." Kai looked confused.

"No way!" said Jenn. "What gave you that idea?"

"When we moved out of the Anquesh communication blackout, we started receiving intelligence from Earth again. Some of the men found reports of an Earth woman given to the Anquesh. It was the price of a treaty between our races."

"It is not a sale," said Kai darkly. "Don't make the mistake of denigrating an Anquera custom solely because you don't have the words in your language to describe it accurately. It is how we make treaties with races we conquer."

"That's the first problem. You haven't conquered anyone!" snapped Oakland. "You need our help!"

"Kai," Jenn whispered. "Please."

"I can't believe you agreed to this!" Oakland wasn't backing down. "You have no problems being as a chip on the bargaining table?"

Jenn stared at him, not knowing what to say. Of course she wasn't okay with her predicament, and she hadn't been from the beginning. But the situation was bigger than herself."

"I don't like it. But things are happening on Earth that you haven't seen on the battlefield. The war has ruined Earth. Most people can't find jobs. The war with Anquera was destroying both our worlds. And the ships you see firing on the Anquesh? They want to kill us all."

"It's not right, Ms. Carden and you know it. I don't care who the Earth wants to sell out to get what it wants. We shouldn't be putting women in slavery. I think you should come with me."

Jenn glanced at Kai. His eyes were growing large, and she saw him starting to flex his muscles. For everyone's sake, she needed to take control of the situation before Kai entered a battle rage.

"Captain Oakland, the Anquesh operate on a strict code of honor. It's part of their culture and one of the reasons why the Earth government was comfortable with the treaty. I promised I would fulfill the agreement between our two peoples as written. You're a soldier; you should do the same thing. As Kai and I are bound together, so are our two peoples bound with each other. They are our allies in a treaty. I suggest you start acting like it."

Jenn wanted to stand as she delivered these words, but she wasn't wearing any pants. Instead, she leaned forward and looked at Oakland with what she hoped was a confident stare.

Oakland looked away from Jenn. Kai still looked like he wanted to rip the Captain's face off. He looked back at Jenn.

"Well, then. I guess I better get back to the ship."

"Wait," Kai interjected. "There is something I want to talk to you about."

Great, thought Jenn. *He's going to talk business while I sit naked behind his desk. I hope he doesn't beat the crap out of this guy.*

"I need more ships," said Kai haughtily. He was still irritated with Oakland.

"There are no more to offer."

"You can still provide something useful, but you haven't realized its value yet. Do you remember the holograms you put in from of us when we first met? We might be able to do interesting things with them. How many can you generate?"

"One per ship at the most."

"Then seven will have to do."

"The holograms consume a good deal of power when they're running. They take away some energy from the weapons system. That's why we used them during our last encounter. You had disabled our lasers, and the only defense we had was to lead you in a different direction with a decoy."

Kai thought about Oakland's revelation. "Even so, it's something the Similcue won't expect. Prepare your ships."

"You've got to be kidding me." Oakland looked incredulous that Kai had the audacity to issue him an order.

"Please," said Jenn. "We need every advantage to fight against the Similcue."

Oakland sighed. "Okay. I'll tell our ships about your plan, and we'll see what we can do."

"Thank you," said Jenn.

"Follow me." Sevit extended his hand and ushered Oakland out the room. As he departed, Sevit looked over his shoulder, letting his gaze linger on Jenn before it drifted to Kai, finally giving him a naughty smile.

"Get going," Kai growled. "My sindare and I have more things to discuss in private."

"I'm sure you do." Kai snorted as the door slammed shut.

Finally given the opportunity to dress herself, Jenn stuck her feet through the ankles of the pantaloons and held up the garment, looking for a way to secure it around her waist.

"Let me help you." He stepped behind the desk and pulled some tabs on either side of her waist. The pants automatically adjusted themselves to Jenn's size.

"You sure know your way around a woman's pantaloons."

"It is familiar territory to an Anquesh warrior like myself," he replied casually.

"You have a lot of experience, then?"

"Don't worry, sindare. I'll always like yours best. You're all set now." He gave her a swat on her ass.

"Hey!" she protested. "So what precisely do you like best? Territory? Or pantaloons?"

He put his arms around her. "Both. Thank you." He rested his forehead against hers. "I noticed you wrapped Oakland around your finger."

"Momma always told me you can catch more flies with honey than with vinegar."

CHAPTER 25

Kai kept his arm around Jenn, holding her tightly while he studied the battle board. He was proud that she had stood up to Oakland and declared her intent to honor the treaty. Sevit looked at her differently now, too. She had earned his respect and Sevit would defend her if anyone from Anquera spoke about her inappropriately. His sindare had the right instincts. Jenn had done her part getting the Earth commander to fight with them. Kai's part was to win the battle.

He ordered the computer to display the magnetic fields surrounding the planets in the solar system. The battle board lit up, showing lines of color surrounding the planets and their rings. He slowly traced the magnetic lines of solar flares from the sun.

The magnetic distribution of the solar system gave information about where the enemy ships could safely move. Although it was possible to make inter-solar jumps, no pilot would want to direct their spaceship too close to a planet or through a flare. The first would send them careening into the atmosphere. The second would burn them to a crisp. Kai made notations on the holographic battle board by tracing his fingers through the fields, crossing out areas the enemy couldn't travel.

There was only one place for them to hide.

"Do you see it?" said Kai.

"Yes, Commander."

"I don't see anything," said Jenn.

"Look here, behind our second moon," Kai said. "They have to be hiding on the far side. The third moon will shield them from solar flares, and the first moon conceals their position."

"I think you're right, Commander. It's the only place that makes sense. If they tried to jump through the other magnetic fields, their ships would be destroyed."

"Can you explain it in English to an Earth girl?"

"All star drives generate magnetic fields. It's similar what you encounter on a planet."

"You mean like when you put two magnets next to each other? Depending on their positions, they stick together, or they repel one another."

"That's correct, depending on the alignment of electrons in the magnetic field. In fact, the ship's propulsion is created through interaction with a magnetic pole."

"So if they're not here, they're going to blow themselves up?"

"If you want to be inelegant about it, yes. The Earth ships should approach the dark side of the moon and project their false holographic ships below the Similcue. We'll come over the top of the moon and trap them between us. Relay the orders to the battle group. Coordinate with the captains and assign them approach vectors."

Jenn was staring intently at the board. "Are you sure this is going to work?"

But before Kai could answer, the communications officer began speaking.

We're receiving a communication from the palace. It's from Emperor Warrel."

"Emperor," Kai said sadly, shaking his head. "Put him on the screen." He escorted Jenn to the center of the bridge.

Warrel had chosen to communicate from the conference room behind the throne. It was the safest room in the palace.

"Commander, I order you to stand down immediately. We have made an agreement with the Similcue." Kai watched shocked as he saw a Similcue ambassador move into view of the camera.

"The promise of one of these dishonorable wretches is worthless. They follow a similar pattern whenever they plan to annihilate a civilization. They make promises they don't intend to keep, and the next thing you know they stab you in the back.

Kai couldn't believe he was having this conversation. How to defend against other alien races was something a first-year Academy cadet would know. The problem was, Warrel never attended the Academy.

"Your words border on insubordination. It's bad enough that you're contemplating treason, but I see you have my fiancee at your side.

"About that," said Jenn. "The wedding's off. I've spent my life looking for a man who wants to keep me happy, not keeping me prisoner."

A few officers aboard the Ruvien chuckled while Warrel's face grew red.

"You will not refuse me, human."

"You had your chance to impress me with your fighting ability and frankly, your Highness, you did not. I'm choosing to go with the original agreement between our people."

"That agreement is no longer in place," Warrel growled.

"Let's be clear about what you're saying. You have no intention of fulfilling the treaty?" Warrel shook his head. "I'm not an expert on Anquera, but tell me something, Kai. Isn't that considered dishonorable? Your Highness, if you have no intention of fulfilling your end of the bargain, we have no need to satisfy ours. It's goodbye for us, Warrel. Better luck next time."

Kai made a hand motion to cut off the communication. Warrel's face faded from the screen as he sputtered over Jenn's monolog.

Jenn looked up at Kai. "I didn't go too far, did I? He looked terribly angry."

"I'm not going to worry about that until my court-martial. We've lost the element of surprise. Send a message to the remaining ships. It's time for us to move!"

The Ruvien and the other ships of the Anquesh fleet made a jump to the second moon in the system. The ships spread out in an arc and slowly moved over the north pole of the moon.

Jenn breathed in sharply when she saw the scene below the Ruvien. Beneath the Similcue ships, were seven United Earth Alliance vessels, like pieces on a three-dimensional chess board.

"Are those the holograms? I can't believe they look real to our eyes and the ship's computers."

In front of them, the Similcue ships fired at the holograms. The shots passed harmlessly through the images.

"The Similcue spacecraft are unable to fire right now while their weapons recharge. We have an opportunity as long as we can move fast enough. Jam their signals. All ships, engage the enemy!"

The Similcue ships were caught in an attack from all sides, receiving blasts from both the United Earth Alliance ships and the Anquesh. A few enemy vessels on the outside of the formation were quickly disabled, but those in the middle had more time to react and used the outer ships as shields. Some moved away to avoid the destruction and others returned fire.

"We've disabled five of the enemy ships. Two Earth ships are critically damaged. Sir, we just lost another spacecraft. It's a total loss. The Similcue spacecraft in our vicinity are surrounding us."

"Stay calm and engage the closest ship in one-on-one combat," commanded Kai. "Don't let up, and don't be afraid."

Jenn didn't need a viewscreen to see the fighting any longer. Flashes of laser fire illuminated the bridge like lightning across the night sky. Suddenly, an enemy show found its target and the Ruvien started shaking. The bridge shifted into a scene of controlled chaos. Different voices reported on damaged sections, shield strength, and casualty estimates.

Kai released Jenn, calling out orders to fire the Ruvien's weapons. The ship vibrated again. Jenn watched a green Similcue ship grow larger as it filled the main viewscreen. It was coming forward at a dangerous rate.

"I think they intend to ram us, Commander."

"Brace for impact."

The Ruvien lurched as the two ships collided. A workstation exploded, starting a fire that threatened to spread around the bridge.

"Jenn, you need to get to my office."

"I'm not going without you."

"It's a secure area, triple-reinforced with a self-contained breathing system. You'll be safe there. I can't work if I'm distracted."

Jenn didn't want to leave Kai. She looked at him, eyes filled with tears and disbelief on her beautiful face. Reluctantly, she started to move to safety.

In front of her, one of the officers fell to the deck. His workstation was burning in an uncontrolled fire. Kai rushed to move him to a secure location, but as he picked up the body, a sickening squeal filled the bridge. A girder started to fall from the ceiling, starting a rain of plastic debris in the bridge.

He couldn't get out of the way in time.

"Kai!" Jenn yelled.

The thick metal beam fell on top of Kai and pain seared his shoulder. He found himself trapped beneath an immovable weight as flames from the workstation licked at the legs of his uniform, burning him. Kai couldn't move, he couldn't breathe, and he was being burned alive.

The last thing he heard was Jenn's voice calling to him. "I'll get you out!"

CHAPTER 26

The world swirled around Kai in a cycle of light and dark. Thoughts came with difficulty and far too slowly to be coherent. The pain was his constant companion though some moments were more painful than others. He was vaguely aware of people moving around him, but he had no idea who they were.

At any rate, it didn't matter. In his more lucid moments, he could remember that he lost a great battle. The Ruvien's bridge was destroyed in flames while he did nothing, trapped helplessly under a fallen beam. Men under his command died in excruciating ways. Some must be prisoners of an enemy who had no concept of honor.

For the first time in Kai's life, he had failed. At this moment, Anquera lay in ruins. His mother was dead. His stepfather was dead, and an idiot sat on the throne.

And Jenn, his sindare? Even if she were alive, she deserved better than a failed warrior.

Raspy sounds came from his raw throat. He was trying to say one thing. "Kill me now."

The noise that came out of his throat was barely recognizable as an intelligent language.

"Doctor!" called a female voice. "I think he's finally awake."

"Commander? Don't try to speak. I had to insert a breathing tube in your throat. Can you move your fingers?"

With effort and a lot of pain Kai, moved the index finger on his right hand.

"Great. Tap once if you understand what I'm saying."

Tap.

"Excellent. You've suffered burns on your legs and arms. Your right thigh bone and hip were fractured. Fire control extinguished the flames eventually, but there was still a lot of damage. We have your arms and legs wrapped in a unique material that will accelerate the healing from the burns. I've turned off the machine. We'll get the tube out of you in a few minutes."

Kai impatiently tapped his fingers.

"Give it a few minutes. Sevit is around somewhere. Do you want to tap with him?"

Tap.

"I'll get him. In the meantime, Jennifer Carden is here to keep you company."

Frantic tapping.

"No? I don't understand. I assure you, she's been by your side the entire time."

Tap tap. Kai didn't want her to see him like this. Weak.

204

"Yes, Kai," Jenn crooned. "I've been here, watching you tap like a madman. I'm not going to leave you."

Kai looked straight to the ceiling. He didn't want to be humiliated further by having his sindare see him like this.

Helpless. Broken. Defeated.

"Commander," said Sevit. "The Ruvien is concealed inside one of the craters of the first moon. We've gone undetected until now, but we think it's because our fleet managed to destroy most of the Similcue ships. The remaining fleet ships are in orbit around the fourth planet while we complete repairs. Rescue operations have started, taking people from critically damaged ships and redeploying them on vessels with less structural damage."

"How many died?" Jenn interjected.

"I'm afraid the casualty count was high. We lost several hundred men, most from the Ruvien. The Similcue ship which rammed into us also tore a hole in our hull. A cascade of problems started after that incident, including venting of the internal atmosphere and an electrical system overload. We're almost ready to start moving again. Should I have us meet the other ships?"

Tap.

"Good. If you'll excuse me, I have some things to check on. I'll be back."

Kai tried to turned his head, but found his movement limited by the wires and tubes.

"He's a good man," said Jenn. "He's been concerned about you."

Tap tap.

"You're tired. Get some sleep. Go ahead. I'll wait right here with you."

Tap tap. Kai had a feeling Jenn couldn't understand his message.

The doctor returned to Kai's bed. "Let's get that tube out."

* * * *

Jenn couldn't remember ever being so glad to see a person regain consciousness. It was hard for her to see Kai wrapped in bandages and a breathing tube in his mouth. It made her feel helpless. She had seen wounded combatants before, of course, but this was different to her.

It was Kai.

She looked around the medical bay, which was now nearly empty. For the past few days, there had been a constant flow of Anquesh soldiers with different injuries. Some had burns, and others had broken bones. None had anything close to the extensive injuries of the Anquesh commander, and he was the only one still recovering.

Kai coughed after the doctor removed the breathing tube.

"Would you like some water?" Jenn held a cup to his lips.

"No," Kai rasped. "Leave me."

She pulled back, confused by the way he was responding to her. She supposed she could cut Kai some slack. He had a horrible experience. His burns must be painful. She'd seen similar injuries working with Earth soldiers and heard their tales of unrelenting pain. No painkillers could relieve the agony. *But I thought my presence would comfort him.*

"Is something the matter?"

"You shouldn't be here."

"The doctor said it was okay for you to have visitors."

He turned his head away. "That's not what I meant."

"What did you mean, then?"

"Go! I'll make sure someone brings you back to one of the Earth ships."

"I don't understand what you're saying."

"I'm saying you should leave and go back to your people. There is no longer a need for you to be with me."

She stared at him blankly. "Kai, you've had a bad experience, but that doesn't mean you need to make a hasty decision."

"We've all had a bad experience. Leave me, Jenn. It's best for everyone this way."

Anger welled up in Jenn's heart. Perhaps she shouldn't have these feelings about an injured alien, but his words cut deeply. She was beginning to believe his feelings for her might be authentic. It had taken a long time for her to think there might be a future for them, and he had decided to send her away.

Of course he was. Why would he do anything differently? She was just a bargaining piece, one that was apparently no longer needed by Anquera.

"If that's what you want, that's what you'll get." She turned and fled from the medical bay, tears stinging her eyes. She ran down the halls, not knowing where she was going, or why. The ship looked empty. She knew it was because everyone was busy making repairs to the ship.

Jenn slowly stopped. Running through the ship wouldn't do her no good. She would have wait until someone came along. Then she could ask them to get Sevit for her. She didn't know how long that would take, but she knew one thing for sure. She would never speak to Kai again.

CHAPTER 27

Jenn made her way to the bridge. The bridge crew looked up when the human entered, unspoken questions in their eyes.

She couldn't take the stares. Her face burned, and her heart was in shambles. Jenn was one breath away from bursting into tears. She rushed through the bridge into Kai's office, which was the only place she knew how to reach. From here, she could ask Sevit to arrange her transport to the Earth command ship.

She sat in the big chair behind Kai's desk and put her head in her hands. When did everything go wrong? Back on earth, when she married Anton instead of tossing the cheating liar out on his ass. At the time, she didn't know about his deception. Jenn had allowed her stupid trusting heart to let Anton spin illusive dreams as he tickled her ears, telling her what she wanted to hear.

Her heart had led her astray once again when she began to fall for the Anquesh warrior. Kai had turned on her too, just like Anton. She wondered why it so important to her for this warrior to desire her? It wasn't like being an alien bride was her idea in the first place. She never expected Kai to choose her. Jenn never wanted to leave Earth. In a few short weeks, her life had been turned upside-down.

There were brief moments when Kai made Jenn feel like he genuinely cherished and cared about her. Sometimes the look in his eyes told her that he wanted her more than anything in the universe. Maybe those moments were what kept her going.

The door opened, and Sevit entered the office, looking at a computer in his hand. He glanced up, surprise registering on his face when he saw Jenn.

"Why are you here? Why aren't you with the commander?"

"He doesn't want me there or anywhere in his vicinity. He told me to go back to my people." She tried to keep her voice level but her breath caught in her throat as she said her last words.

Sevit's expression became neutral. He looked like a soldier who had been given an order he disagreed with, but could not disobey.

"Stay here," said Sevit. "I'll return in a few minutes."

When he left, Jenn was alone in Kai's office again. She looked around the room. On the right, trophies were carefully stored behind a clear, glass-like material. It couldn't be glass because it would have shattered during the attack on the ship. Behind the transparent wall, the trophies had been jostled from their places, some leaning against the glass and others at different angles on their sides.

The sheer number of them were impressive. Kai must have collected them his entire life. She stared at them, taking in the various pieces that represented moments of a warrior's life, and realized something.

Kai had never lost a single battle before.

The insight washed over her like a cold spring rain. Of course. For a man that had never lost before, getting injured in a single battle would seem like a massive failure.

She had seen this mentality before in her patients, especially the ones who identified with the warrior mythos. They went into battle convinced they were wielding a shield of invulnerability. The mindset gave them protection against the horrors of the battlefield. It helped them overcome challenges through training, skill, and sheer will.

That was the theory. Laser blasts went right through the mental invulnerability shields. When a weapon came at them which tore their bodies to shreds, their psychological defenses crumbled. Jenn's job wasn't merely helping soldiers heal their bodies. She needed to mend their minds and assist soldiers when they tried to overcome their sense of failure. And this was in a society where men had career options other than fighting.

Things were different on Anquera. From what she could see, the Anquesh concept of what it meant to be a man was intertwined with the notion of being a warrior. Powerful in battle. Acting with honor. Fulfilling one's duty. Dividing enemies into strict categories, like honored and hated.

They send Kai to Earth to fulfill a contract of honor, one that rested on centuries of Anquera tradition and law. He followed orders out of a sense of duty to his planet.

211

With a shock, she realized Kai probably never wanted to go to Earth at all and had never desired a human wife.

When he met her, he had said something about *those abominable women.* No, there was nothing about Earth women he liked. He must have selected her because he was tired of the process and everything to be over. He would take an Earth woman as his wife back to Anquera, perform the minimum required to respect the treaty, then go back to his life as a warrior.

Then what would happen to Jenn? She didn't know the kind of life she'd have, but she imagined it would be lonely and isolated as a single blonde in a world of tall, dark-haired people.

Uncertainty swirled through Jenn's head, making her feel confused emotions. For a moment, her insight into Kai's behavior had almost made her feel centered again. But she had no idea what to do after thinking about Kai's motivations.

Everything made her angry. How dare he? How dare he and this group of alien bastards take her from Earth for political purposes, then throw her away at the first opportunity. How dare he tell her to go away.

How dare he kiss her with such passion and then act like it was nothing.

Jenn stood, feeling like there was a fire in her soul. She was going to give Kai a piece of her mind before he shipped her off like a piece of trash.

High on fury and rage, she strode out of the Anquesh Commander's office, ignoring the stares of the warriors surrounding her. She held her head high walking with confident steps to the Ruvien's medical bay.

* * * *

"What did you say to Jenn Carden?"

Kai withheld a groan. His second-in-command made the question sound like a challenge.

"Go away, Sevit."

"No, I will not. When exactly did you think it would be a good idea to get the Earth representative angry?"

Different thoughts tumbled through Kai's mind as he tried to process Sevit's words. To everyone else, Jenn was merely an Anquesh treaty prize.

He hadn't expected she would be his sindare. He hadn't expected he would fall in love with her.

Everything Kai wanted to say to Sevit sounded like the words of a petulant child in his head, so he decided to stare at the ceiling instead as Sevit continued talking.

"Don't you understand we need her more now than ever before? She is the Emperor's chosen visible symbol of our treaty with Earth. We can use her as a rallying point. Our people can gather around her to make things right again."

Kai sighed. Sevit didn't know that the Emperor was against the treaty from the beginning, but Kai would not dishonor his memory with the revelation.

"They defeated us." Kai's throat was still raw from smoke inhalation.

"They did not. At worst, they fought us to a draw, but it was not a defeat."

"A draw," Kai said derisively, turning his head away.

"They had more ships than us. We did well, all things considered."

"Doing well is a euphemism for losing. Where were the rest of our ships? What's our plan for the future? They'll just come back, and with bigger numbers the next time."

Jenn pulled away the curtain from around Kai's bed. "Do you know what you need to do for the future? Stop feeling sorry for yourself."

"Sevit, get her out of here."

"If you touch me, I'll make what happened to Warrel look like I was fucking him."

"Yes, ma'am," said Sevit, stepping back with his arms raised in the air.

"And you!" she exclaimed, turning her attention to Kai. "You suffered a defeat. Big deal. Alien up and deal with it!"

Kai stared at her, shock written over his face.

"You think you're the first person in the universe who suffered a set-back? I've seen warriors with serious injuries. Paralysis. Amputation. Hell, multiple amputees don't feel as sorry for themselves as you do right now. If we had the time, I would leave you alone. Eventually, you would realize how ridiculous your thoughts are. But we don't have the luxury of time right now. A bunch of ships waiting in space for you to lead them, Kai. I'm not going to leave until you get out of bed and remember you're a member of the Anquesh Empire's royal house."

CHAPTER 28

A week had passed since the battle, and Kai was feeling better this morning. It helped that Jenn had just massaged his skin with burn cream. The prickling feeling in his healing skin had settled down, but he knew it would come back with a vengeance later in the day.

He lay face down on the bed, which was both comfortable and practical. Jenn's hands moving over his body were making him react unpredictably. Kai shifted his body, trying to take pressure off his growing erection. If she didn't slow down, he was going to make an embarrassing mess on the sheets.

Her hands felt soft and smooth, like a piece of silk on his skin. They were strong and knew where to soften the knots in his muscles. She pressed and worked the pressure points until he felt like a relaxed puddle of goo in the sheets.

"The balm from your doctor is amazing," Jenn said. She had constantly been talking, but he only paid attention to half of the words she said. "I think it makes my hands look young. I bet I could repackage it as a face cream and sell it on Earth. I would make millions."

"What's a face cream?" groaned Kai as she hit another tight spot.

"It's a topical ointment to help women look beautiful."

"That's silly. Women don't need creams to make them more attractive to their mates. You certainly don't."

"We use them anyway."

"Anquesh women do not."

"Maybe you just don't know about it. Women like to look beautiful for men. Your skin has already shed the burnt outer layer, and there is nice healthy new skin underneath. You won't have any noticeable scars, which is amazing. I can only imagine what it would do for aging skin. I know a bunch of older nurses who would give up their retirement funds for something this good."

Kai realized something. "You can't wait to get to Earth, can you?" His heart sank as he spoke the words out loud.

Jenn's hands stopped and rested on his back. "Come on. We've got to work your leg now."

"I don't want to," he moaned. For one thing, he'd rather have Jenn's hands on his body than do work. For another, he didn't want to turn over and reveal his arousal to her face.

A doctor poked his head out from behind a curtain. "Nurse Jenn," he said. "We have another injured soldier who could use your help."

Kai restrained a growl. Once the doctors learned Jenn knew physical therapy, they enlisted her to help bedridden warriors recover faster. He was proud that she was willing to help his men, but he didn't like to imagine her hands on any of them.

Jenn pulled up a blanket over Kai. "Even if you don't want to show me, I know it's there. I'll be back."

Kai melted into the sheets as her footsteps faded into the background. He felt relaxed and for the first time in days, he felt no pain, but he needed to do something about the throbbing between his legs. It pulsed insistently. All he needed was a few minutes to work his hand under and stroke his cock.

The thought of Jenn being near him, touching and flooding him with the pleasure of her hands was practically overwhelming.

"Commander."

The voice startled him like a bucket of cold water.

"Yes, Sevit," said Kai with exasperation.

"I'm sorry to disturb you, but we've detected some unusual activity on our sensors. We're not sure what it is, but you should know. The readings suggest a ship is following us."

Kai turned suddenly and looked directly at Sevit. "Help me out of here. I want to see the information with my own eyes and I'm going to get out of this damned hospital bed. Get my crutches and help me up, or I'll crawl there by myself."

Jenn had urged the engineering crew to construct a set of crutches custom-fitted for Kai, according to her specifications. Jenn thought it was peculiar that Anquera didn't have any devices to help patients with their recovery process. Anquesh warriors recovered from their injuries quickly, or not at all. The only treatment prescribed for the injured was bed rest.

Jenn thought it was ridiculous.

"You'll lose muscle mass that way and make your recovery take longer. It doesn't matter how quickly you heal." When she had first presented him with the crutches, he pushed them away. Jenn didn't give up. Even when Kai screamed in pain, she made him get out of bed and walk around.

Kai would never admit it to Jenn, but he felt like he was healing more quickly than usual. He slipped a shirt over his head, wincing as the fabric slid over the sensitive flesh.

Sevit watched Kai move his immobilized leg over the side of the bed and put the crutches under his arm. He tipped forward, carefully easing his working leg onto the floor.

"I don't think this is a good idea. It's not an approved medical treatment," said Sevit doubtfully.

"I've been walking around here the past few days. I'm tired of sitting in bed on my butt."

"Maybe I should consult with the doctor first."

"You will not, and that's an order. You should come with me and assist if necessary."

Kai hobbled out the door slightly ahead of Sevit. He moved faster than he normally did. Once Kai became accustomed to the motion of the crutches, it felt like his body was moving forward on a swing rather than walking. Kai was glad to get out of the medical bay, and he had big plans. His cabin beckoned. He was going to sleep in his bed tonight.

When Kai entered the bridge, the words "Officer on deck" sounded like music to his ears. He looked like a mess wearing hospital clothing, wielding the crutches, and appearing disheveled. He didn't care.

He moved to the sensor station. Like the rest of the bridge, it looked battle-worn and still had visible fire damage. Someone had moved the beam which fell on Kai.

"Show me what you've got," said Kai.

A short video played, displaying the positions of the stars. He didn't see anything unusual until the end of the scene. One of the stars blinked and disappeared.

"What's the latest intelligence we have about the Similcue? Do they have cloaking technology, like the humans?"

"Not to our knowledge. That information is exclusive to Earth."

"Call Oakland. I need to speak with him as soon as possible."

Kai stormed into his office. He went to his desk, lowered himself into his seat, and propped his crutches on the wall behind him. Oakland's image appeared on a viewscreen in front of him.

"Which one of your ships is following us?" demanded Kai. "The Anquesh deal harshly with spies."

"I'm not sure what you mean. We know the positions of all our vessels, and none of them are tracking you."

"There's a cloaked ship behind us, Oakland. Only Earth ships have the technology."

"That's not entirely accurate," Oakland mumbled.

"You didn't give it to anyone, did you? Like a race who has declared war on both our planets?" rumbled Kai. He was quickly losing patience with the human.

"We thought they were our allies. They shared technology with us. We made improvements, and gave the improvements to them in return."

"Gods!" Kai slammed his hand onto the desk.

"We weren't aware they could implement it this quickly. Our analysts thought the Similcue were slow in adopting new technology."

"It takes them a while because they don't usually create it. They steal it. But you handed it to them on a silver platter, with instructions."

"We didn't know what would happen. We thought we could use them." Oakland stopped speaking. He had said too much already.

"You wanted to use them?" Kai said incredulously.

"You have to understand. We didn't trust the Similcue, but they could make us powerful."

"So you pretended to be their ally?"

"We got what we needed from them, but that doesn't mean we trusted them. At the time, we were in the middle of war with Anquera. If they saw us offer a treaty..."

"They would have the perfect time to attack when our defenses were down!" roared Kai.

"That's right. When you destroyed each other, our plan was to mop up the pieces." Oakland turned to look at Kai in the eyes. "We were at war, Commander. We were prepared to do whatever it took to win."

"Answer one question for me. Did you ever intend to fulfill the treaty, or was reneging on it part of the plan?"

"I wasn't part of all the discussions. The treaty was only one of many possibilities when I left Earth. We never thought the United Earth Alliance would approve of the requirements. Your provision for an Earth bride sounded ridiculous."

"In the planning, what was going to happen to Jenn?"

Oakland's face turned white. "Since Ms. Carden cooperated with the enemy, she would be tried as a war criminal. The UEA will disavow the treaty and Jenn's actions. They don't want to be the ones who sold a woman into slavery."

CHAPTER 29

Kai felt his muscles tighten and his mind being to cloud up as the nuxmunit took over his body. He shivered, trying to regain control of himself. He didn't need to go into a battle rage with a hologram. But he was infuriated by the idea that Jenn's people would use her, then discard her when they didn't need her any longer.

"We'll talk later," he snapped, ending the communication. He was shaking by this point, feeling sick to his stomach. He leaned back in his chair and closed his eyes. He was early in the nuxmunit cycle, and could still call upon years of training to calm himself. Finally, he felt the anger drain away. He lay his head back onto the headrest.

These were certainly dishonorable people. But were the Emperor's plans any better, even though they were at war with each other?

The treaty was turning into a mess. An absolute disaster. Kai's journey to Earth would deliver Jenn into the hands of predators. Was there a way out?

Kai shook his head, wondering how they got into such a predicament.

There wasn't an obvious solution. The Anquera government was fragmented. Emperor Kanton's death had left a hole in the Empire that Warrel couldn't repair. Kai didn't blame a father for hoping that his son could replace him, but it was evident that Warrel didn't have the right qualities to lead.

They were stuck with him because he was the Emperor's only son.

At best, the nobles could reign in the worst of Warrel's excesses. That strategy might have worked at another time in history, but not now, when Anquera was fighting a war on two fronts. One enemy was merely a problem. Two enemies might be insurmountable.

Kai realized he had to make the humans honor the treaty agreement. Peace would reduce the number of battlefronts, and they would be able to benefit from mutual technology exchange.

But what about Jenn? How was he going to get her to go along with the plan? She didn't feel the same pull to him as he did. They were different species, and their biological responses were mismatched. How could he bridge the gap?

The door to his office opened, but his eyes remained closed. He didn't feel like hearing another devastating message.

"Kai? What are you doing out of bed?"

Jenn's voice was soft and sweet. The sound of his sindare was music to his ears. He opened his eyes slowly and took in her beauty. She was breathtaking.

"I'm looking for you," he said. He didn't feel sorry for the lie, and at the moment, he wasn't sure how much of his statement was false. A part of him knew she would materialize, wherever he was, and drag him back to the medical bay.

She scoffed. "Of course you were. I spend a lot of time in your office. That's the first place I would look too."

Kai noticed that his office looked remarkably tide after a battle. Everything was in its proper place, even the trophies. The maintenance crew would be busy performing repairs on the ship, not spending time cleaning up an office. Had she been in his office rearranging things?

"Come here," he said huskily, motioning with his hand.

"Why?" she said. "Do you need help with something?"

"You could say that."

Jenn walked toward him cautiously with suspicion in her eyes.

"Closer." He reached out his hand. She grasped his hand, intending to lift him out of his seat, but instead he pulled on her arm and swung her body, making her fall on his chest.

"Isn't that better?" he purred. He held her tightly as she squirmed.

"Let me go!"

He bent his head down to her neck and kissed it, then sucked on her skin, making sure to mark her.

"I've been thinking. Do I care about the state of the Earth treaty? I can claim you as my battle prize."

"No, you can't."

"Sure, if you beat me in the marriage ceremony."

Jenn tried to push away, but Kai's grip was too strong.

"Now hold on a second, mister," she sputtered.

"To be precise, it's 'my lord'."

"You're not my lord or anything like it," snapped Jenn.

"You wouldn't have to call me 'my lord,' if we married. Not in private. In public, you would need to meet certain expectations. But I would call you 'my lady'. It all balances out. I think it sounds nice. Lady Imwaden. How does that sound to you?"

"I don't know," she stammered. "On Earth, we don't have to take our husband's name."

Kai licked the base of her throat, then nuzzled her chin. It tickled. He hadn't shaved yet and had a day's growth of beard.

"We can discuss everything later after the ceremonial battle. Assuming I defeat you, we can negotiate everything in the marriage contract." He pulled her into his lap and positioned her arms around his neck. He loved the feeling of her breasts pressing into his chest.

"Marriage contract?"

227

"Sure. Don't you have them on Earth? It clarifies what I will do for you, and what you will do for me."

Kai resumed his explorations of her neck, discovering that she squirmed whenever he sucked lightly on her back, below her hairline. It felt like she was melting into him.

"Did you know you are delicious? Every part of you is sweet."

Kai lifted her shirt to reveal the milky globes of her breasts. He circled his thumbs around each nipple, making them peak into hardness. He bent his head and sucked one in his mouth, gently biting. Jenn gasped while her breathing sped up.

He let his tongue circle the nub, feeling his cock starting to swell beneath her. The sensation of her lovely ass pressing on him was too much for him. He needed to be inside her. Picking at the waistband of her pants, he slid his hand toward her sex. Jenn's wet heat greeted his fingers immediately. He stroked the soft flesh tenderly, almost eagerly, searching for a passionate response. More of her juices spilled onto his hand, and he could only imagine how hot and wet her pussy would feel around his cock.

He wasn't going to play around any longer. It was time to take her.

"I want you," he whispered into her ear. Kai gently licked behind it, drawing mewling noises from her lips as he stroked her with his fingers.

"Then take me," Jenn murmured. She pulled away, and stood up, stretching her arms. Her top came off first, followed by her pants. Kai observed every movement, thinking she was the most attractive creature he had ever seen.

Jenn pulled at the tie string of his medical bay pants and pulled them off, lifting his hips from the chair. She stared at his cock. It was hard, throbbing slightly, and leaking pre-cum from the tip.

"I don't know," she said. "I've never..." Jenn's voice trailed off as her eyes went wide. She couldn't believe what she saw.

"Come here, Jenn," Kai said in a husky voice. He positioned her body so his cock rested between her legs. Her liquid heat spread between them, making his cock slick as she ground against him.

"That's enough for now," he said. "That's amazing. I love feeling you against me. The sensation of silken folds over his hot cock made him want to thrust into her, but he felt twinges of pain in his hip, which was still healing. Their position wasn't going to work if Kai wanted to move energetically.

Jenn arched her back, and he had an idea. He pushed the chair forward to rest her ass on the desk. Jenn looked down as Kai pulled her legs to the armrest. Grasping his cock, he pressed around her sex, teasing her with it.

She whimpered.

Kai thrust forward, the triangular head of his cock piercing her entrance and reaching to her core. He felt more hot wetness surge over his body.

"See," he said in a low voice. "We can do this."

He got to his feet, resting his full weight on his arms. Jenn grasped his cock between her hands, holding him at her entrance.

"Take what you want, sindare," he said. "It's all for you."

She pulled him in. He couldn't help thrusting deeply into her, filling her to the hilt. She moved slowly but murmured words of encouragement. "Yes," she said. "That's good, right there. I need it."

There was more to his little sindare than he would have thought. When their pubic bones touched, she put one leg on his good hip and started rocking, sending waves of pleasure through him. He couldn't stop now. It felt too good.

Jenn gasped. Her sex pulsed around him as she bucked her hips. "Kai!" she screamed.

In the throws of her pleasure, Kai couldn't hold back. White heat seared through his body, and he came deep inside her.

"Sindare!" he called, shuddering with the intensity of his release as he burst apart.

CHAPTER 30

Jenn was frustrated. She hadn't seen Kai for days. She was tired of looking at the group of United Earth Alliance representatives across the table, and she thought they didn't want to see her either.

Ever since the arrival of the combined Anquesh and Earth fleet, neither she nor Kai had been able to convince the UEA that a threat loomed on the horizon. The Similcue were probably on their way to Earth.

She had no idea how Kai was doing, and she missed him. Maybe absence did make the heart grow fonder. She had realized something.

Jenn was in love with the alien warrior. She hadn't been able to tell him about her epiphany, and something inside her would ache until she confessed.

The United Earth Alliance looked at her like she had done something wrong.

"It's not that complicated, and I don't think saying the same thing for the millionth time will convince you. The Similcue have been playing us for fools. They're done toying with Earth. They're going to conquer it. Our technological advancements make us attractive as a slave state."

"What we don't understand, Ms. Carden, is why you are determined to support an alien race which has been humanity's bitter enemy for years."

"You sent me out there! You told me I would be court-martialed and thrown into prison if I didn't fulfill the provisions of the Anquesh treaty."

"We didn't intend for you to sleep with the enemy. You were supposed to play along."

"No one said anything like that to me. Are you finally going to tell me where Kai is?"

"Who?"

"Commander Imwaden!"

"Oh, the alien. I didn't realize you were on a first-name basis with him. Don't worry. We have him secured."

"What does that mean? Is he behind bars?"

"Of course. He is a war criminal."

"Kai's the farthest thing from a war criminal. He has more honor than anyone sitting at this table!"

"Ms. Carden, I'll give you a warning. You need to consider your tone of voice and your audience."

There was a commotion at the door. "Let me in. I'm her lawyer." A tall man with graying hair appeared, dressed in an expensive-looking suit. He pushed his way past the military guard. Jenn thought he looked familiar.

"This is a military proceeding," said one of the officers.

"Military or civil, my client has the right to representation. I'm sorry for being late, Jenn." He sat down in the seat next to her. His hand moved quickly under the desk, so fast she barely noticed it.

"Who are you?"

The man tossed a business card across the table. "Adam Walters, of Kellem, Brace and Walters. My firm is representing Miss Carden. We have a communication protocol. When she failed to call us, we knew we had to do some investigating. You're not playing fair, gentlemen. I almost had to take legal action. But since I found her in your military installation, we can dispense with the pleasantries. Is my client charged with a crime, or is she free to go?"

"Not yet."

"Great. Let's go, Jenn. We're leaving." He stood and put his arm under Jenn, forcefully insisting that she get up as well.

"Wait a minute. You can't do that!"

Adam smiled. "Watch me." He pulled Jenn from the table and pressed his hands together.

The table exploded.

"Time to run." Adam pushed the guard out of the way as he and Jenn ran out of the door into the hallway.

"Who are you?" she gasped.

"We met once before. Tellen. You know me as Tellen. A transport ship is waiting for us. We spotted the Similcue near the planet you call Pluto. They can be here in a single jump."

"What about Kai?"

"I've sent someone to retrieve him."

Jenn ran behind Tellen. No alarms rang in the corridors. In fact, there was no noise anywhere. At the entrance, Jenn found more unconscious soldiers. As she moved to look at them, she heard footsteps behind her. She looked back, a ball of fear enveloping her gut.

Two tall dark-haired men ran out of the darkened hallway. One had a slight limp. It was Kai.

When he saw Jenn, we became energized and ran faster. "Sindare!" He swept Jenn into his arms when he reached her.

"Let's go, Commander," said Tellen. "Time is against us. We should board the transport. Be forewarned, the cloaking system is engaged."

The group ran across a black parking lot as the hot sun beat down on them. As they were about to enter the transport's gaping black maw, rifle shots whizzed over their heads. The bullets bounced off the invisible spaceship.

"Halt!" an Earth soldier called.

Jenn raced into the dark hole. Once her eyes had adjusted to the darkness, she realized they were inside an Anquesh transport. Tellen pushed a button to close the hatch.

"Take off!"

The transport lurched violently, and Jenn fell against a bulkhead as the ship rose into the air. Kai reached out to steady her, and she fell into his arms. It felt good to be surrounded by Kai again.

She opened her mouth to confess her feelings. She didn't know if she would get another chance. Tellen spoke before she could say anything.

"I have made contact with Captain Oakland. He has his ships and several other battle groups ready to break Earth ranks and follow us. He knows what the Similcue can do. I believe the direct quote is, 'If the idiots at UEA can't see the forest for the trees, maybe it's time to chop down the forest.'"

"Humans need to learn to say what they mean," Kai said, looking directly at Jenn.

"It's a little beyond us, I think," she replied with a smile.

"Oakland told me there would be consequences for Jenn's participation in the treaty."

"What consequences? I just did what they told me to do!"

"According to Oakland, they were going to put you in prison on a manufactured charge. You were an uncomfortable and inconvenient reminder of their behavior."

The questions in the conference room made sense now. They were letting her speak as much as she wanted, giving her enough rope to let her say anything they could interpret as treason.

"I guess I can't go home again. We're going to get married. I don't have a choice." Jenn sighed.

"I thought we already agreed there was going to be a wedding, as long as I can beat you in the arena."

"It wasn't an agreement. More like a temporary acquiescence in exchange for certain favors."

"Are you saying I haven't won you yet?" Kai had a sly smile on his face.

"Excuse me, but we're still running a military operation here," Tellen interjected. "We will dock with the Ruvien soon, and we need to have the battle plan against the Similcue worked out. We've had some preliminary meetings with the leaders of the United Earth Alliance. When we arrive on the Ruvien, it's time to have a conference with our allies."

The ship lurched and all forward motion stopped. "We're here already." A hatch opened automatically. "I will take Jenn to your quarters."

"No, Tellen. She's going to stay with me."

Tellen nodded, and they swiftly navigated through the ship's corridors until they reached the bridge of the Ruvien.

When Kai entered, the officers snapped to attention. Kai nodded his head. "At ease. Sevit, what's the situation?"

"We have seven ships that are battle-ready. Captain Oakland and three other Earth captains are ready to speak to you over the communications systems." Sevit passed over a hand-held computer. "These are our battle plans."

Kai took the computer and started rifling his fingers through pages of documents. "Can we put it on the battle board? What do the simulations say?"

"Commander, if the Similcue don't bring any extra ships, I think we have a chance."

Kai lifted his eyebrow. "One chance, Lieutenant?"

"I'm being conservative in my estimates. We might have two chances."

"How about the choke point you identified?"

"Their fourth planet, Mars, doesn't have a magnetic field and is the perfect place for them to conceal themselves.

"Is there any other place they can jump?"

"Yes, that's the second chance. The second planet doesn't have a magnetic field, but it is relatively close to the sun. Solar flares are active."

"Let's head for Mars. Maybe we'll get lucky."

CHAPTER 31

Kai organized a defense of the solar system with Oakland and the other United Earth Alliance captains. Five ships were left between the moon and Earth to provide a failsafe. His navigator gave coordinates for both Mars and Venus to every ship.

"Hold on, Jenn," said Kai. "Interplanetary jumps can be a little rough."

He kept his arm protectively around her should when he gave the order. Twenty-five battle cruisers moved together, a mixture of Anquera and Earth ships. Jenn felt her stomach lurch and in an instant, Earth vanished from the viewscreen. Nothing was visible for several seconds. The bridge crew waited, holding their breaths. Without warning, the electronics came back online, and the screen displayed an image of the red planet spinning underneath them.

"Implement radio silence and turn off all electronic systems," ordered Kai. "Let's go quiet."

Lights dimmed in the bridge, and audio alerts were turned off. No one spoke.

Kai sat in the captain's chair and pulled Jenn into his lap. She blushed looked around the bridge, watching for signs of disapproval from his crew. It seemed like a terrible protocol breach. Thankfully, the soldiers kept their eyes on either their workstations or the display screens.

Kai brushed his lips against her face. "How are you feeling, sindare?" he whispered.

She leaned her head close to his ear. Her chance was now. "I love you, Kai Imwaden."

But Kai wasn't listening to her. The screen held his complete attention. Jenn up to see Similcue ships appearing above Mars.

"Activate the weapons, and commence firing!" Kai shouted.

Laser fire burned jagged streaks into the Similcue ships. They returned fire immediately. So many bright flashes filled the screen that Jenn had to turn her head away to protect her eyes. Kai stood, relinquishing his chair to Jenn. He walked to the battle board to observe the action. He shouted orders into a headset, moving ships into different positions.

"Sir!" someone shouted out. "The Similcue have breached our landing bay. The enemy has boarded the Ruvien!"

"Vent the bay into space."

"It's too late for that, sir. They are in our corridors already."

"Jenn, secure yourself in my office."

She looked around the bridge. The Anquesh soldiers were preparing for battle and distributing weapons to each other, checking them, and arming them to kill.

"Now would be a good time. You might not get another chance."

She didn't want leave, but she didn't want to distract him either. Jenn ran to the office with a heavy heart. She wasn't concerned for her safety, but for Kai's. He had been through too much, too fast. Kai had barely healed from his previous injuries and still walked with a limp. Did he have the strength to fight off another attack?

Jenn sat at the chair behind Kai's desk. It was a place of memories already. She chuckled thinking about the day she sat behind it half-nude. Remembering the day they made love made her yearn for Kai's touch again.

She wondered if he would survive to touch her again.

* * * *

Kai stood in the middle of the bridge. He had ordered the warriors to stay as close to the workstations as possible. The workstations would help conceal his team as the attackers entered the room. Kai's gun was drawn and pointing forward. He was ready to take the first shots on anyone he saw. Kai would draw fire while his men overcome the enemy.

That was the plan, at least.

"Sir, the Similcue fleet has withdrawn. We managed to disable half their ships."

"Excellent." Despite Kai's calm outward appearance, his heart blazed with anger. The cowards had sent a suicide force to engage his team and wreak havoc while their fleet escaped. Kai would hunt down every single one of the bastards who threatened his sindare's home.

Some of the humans he had met were cowardly liars ready to hand over a defenseless female as a faux peace offering, but there were good people on Earth as well. They included Jenn's friend Nayla, Bretland, who gave his life honorably, or even Oakland, who defied a terrible command to save his people. They all lived a life of caring concern for others. There was honor in these humans, and they deserved help against the Similcue.

The bridge hatch blew open. Kai fired his gun wildly, pumping multiple laser blasts into the enemy bodies, taking down as many as he could. These Similcue, being suicide warriors, had no concern for their lives and were willing to die as long as they took down an Anquesh warrior with them. Kai dropped down to the deck to avoid the laser blasts but felt pain in different parts of his body. He had taken down a few Similcue, but they kept coming.

Kai wasn't defending the bridge by himself. His men were firing as well, and one by one the Similcue warriors fell to the ground. Soon the firing stopped, and all the Similcue were dead.

He breathed a sigh of relief and tried to sit up, but found that couldn't. For some reason, he felt weak.

Sevit appeared at his side. "Get someone from medical right away. The commander has multiple wounds."

* * * *

For the second time in as many weeks, Jenn looked down at Kai in a hospital bed. Various tubes and wires protruded from his body. Kai's eyes were closed, and he was as still as death.

"After you recover, we're going to find you another job. This one is bad for my mental health."

Aden and Tellen walked to Kai's bed. "How is the Commander?" asked Tellen quietly.

"We can only wait," said Jenn. "They've done everything possible."

"Who would have known your people had such advanced surgical techniques?" Tellen asked.

"Aden did."

"I was supposed to learn as much about Earth as I could. And you put everything on television! I couldn't believe people watch surgeries for entertainment. Our doctors have different healing techniques."

"You were the only one who thought to ask Earth's doctors for assistance."

"They seemed happy to help."

Oakland had called the United Earth Alliance immediately to tell them of the Similcue's attack. He also mentioned who devised the battle plan which defeated them. Being politically savvy, Oakland made sure the Anquesh fleet and Earth news organizations were monitoring the transmission. In the face of a public announcement of Anquera's value as an ally, the United Earth Alliance had to announce the treaty between Earth and Anquera was valid.

But it would only remain valid if Kai stayed alive.

Suddenly all the energy rushed out of Jenn's body, and she felt like she had to sit down. "If you don't mind, I'd like to spend some time alone with Kai."

"Of course, my lady," said Tellen.

"I'll just be outside the curtain," said Aden. "I'm here for security."

"I didn't ask the question. I knew already. Kai requires a guard."

"You don't understand," said Tellen. "I'm here for the Commander's protection. Aden is here for yours. I'll be in the hallway on patrol." He nodded his head and strode out of the medical bay.

"You're here to protect me?"

"Yes, Lady Imwaden."

It was strange how quickly the Anquesh assumed she was Kai's wife. They hadn't even had the ceremony yet.

"May I approach?" Jenn could easily recognize Sevit's voice by now. "How is our commander?"

"It was difficult, but he'll recover. They had to insert some stents into the damaged arteries. They doctors said one artery had such extensive damage that they couldn't believe he was still alive. Kai lost a lot of blood."

"We have plenty of volunteers ready to donate."

"I don't think they'll be necessary. We use a combination of artificial blood and nanites to accelerate the healing. It's better for a high-risk surgery."

What Jenn didn't say was that the doctors were unsure how Anquesh physiology would handle Earth medicine. They had warned her that Kai's body could reject the stents or the nanites. Kai was on the cutting edge of Anquesh medical research.

"If we had known your people had this much science, we would have conquered you sooner." Sevit smiled. Jenn understood the joke, but she wasn't in a particularly humorous mood.

"Is there something I can do for you, Sevit?"

"First, I wanted to congratulate you for being officially designated ambassador to Anquera. The Earth government made an excellent choice."

"Thank you. I was just in the right place at the right time."

"No, Lady Imwaden, I sincerely mean it. You will do well in your new position."

Jenn bit her tongue. *I don't know about that,* she thought. *It's more like the United Earth Alliance had no idea how to deal with Anquera and was ready to send anyone who seemed vaguely qualified.*

"We are scheduled to arrive at Anquera in ten days."

"Do you know what we're going to find there?"

"No one does. Whatever it is, I'm confident the additional ships from Earth us will help us handle the situation."

Did he intend to use the Earth ships to stop a civil war? Jenn was pretty sure that wasn't the intended purpose. Ten days would feel like a lifetime. Would Kai be next to her, or would she be burying him in an Anquesh ritual?

The thought was too awful to contemplate.

CHAPTER 32

"Hey, soldier," said a familiar voice. "You really should wake up. You've been off the ventilator for an hour now."

Kai was on the edge of consciousness, floating in a timeless state. He couldn't put his finger on the last thing he remembered, and he didn't want to.

"Let me sleep."

"You've slept for three days. Now it's time to wake up."

Kai's eyes fluttered open. He struggled to focus his eyes. When he could see again, he found Jenn's sweet face leaning over the bed.

"You know," said Jenn, "if you were human you would be walking around the next day after your operation. We made allowances for an alien."

"Humans are a fearsome race, even if you are diminutive."

"We have a song about that somewhere. Short people will they get you every time."

"I am sure your music contains with cultural references about how wonderful humans are, just like every other civilization. Can I have some water?"

"Are you trying to sweet-talk me into getting you some water?"

247

"Do I have to do more? I'm exhausted."

Jenn made a little gasp which she tried to hide by covering her mouth with her hand. Jenn didn't cover her eyes, and Kai saw tears gathering at the corners.

"Why are you crying, sindare? I'm right here."

"I almost lost you, again." She held a cup to his lips with a straw, wiping her eyes with her hands. "You've got to stop these near-death experiences. I can't take the stress."

He took a few sips, then pushed the cup away.

"I'll make you a promise. I'll stop almost dying."

"That's fine, as long as you don't start dying."

Kai laughed briefly but stopped when the movement inundated his body with pain.

"What kind of surgery did I have?"

"Heart surgery."

"We don't have surgeries for hearts," he said, wondering if she was teasing him again.

"The Anquesh might not, but my people certainly do. Human doctors operated on you. Between Earth medicine and the Anquesh healing speed, you should be back to normal in a couple of weeks."

"It feels like my chest was cut open."

"It was. You should see the surgical saws. They are *enormous*. Any of you people who sees one will marvel at your bravery for enduring it. You don't have to tell them you were asleep when they cut you open."

"Humans are annoying. Come here."

"Why? What are you going to do to me?"

"I'm going to shut that pretty mouth of yours."

"How do you plan to do that?"

"Simple." Kai pulled her sharply to him and kissed her passionately. Gods, he was grateful to be alive. Her lips were luscious and tender. Kai wanted to ravish her mouth. In the end, Jenn broke away.

"Easy there, soldier. You aren't cleared for active duty yet."

"Consider that a down payment for next time."

"Don't worry. You owe me the balance plus interest." She gave him a quick kiss. "Get some rest. I need something to eat. Suddenly I feel ravenous."

"Wait a minute. You woke me up to tell me to go back to sleep?"

She laughed. "Of course. You're in a hospital, aren't you?"

* * * *

A few days after his surgery, Kai stood on the bridge of the Ruvien, watching the approach to Anquera. Jenn stood beside him, hooking her arm around his waist. She was ready to support him if he suddenly felt weak. It seemed like he was regaining his strength quickly. Jenn knew his rapid recovery was related to her post-operative ministrations. Kai was slowly beginning to realize there were things about Jenn he would have to accept. One of them was her dedication to caring for the sick and injured.

There were no Similcue ships around Anquera. On the trip, Kai had sent inquiries to various posts through the empire. No one reported seeing any enemy vessels.

The Anquesh had beaten back an enemy and made a valuable ally. On any other day, they would be preparing to celebrate.

But Jenn wasn't getting a feeling of happiness from the crew. There weren't any Anquesh ship around the planet either, and the palace wasn't answering their communications. The world appeared uninhabited.

"We'll have to go down in person," said Kai with a sigh. The last thing he wanted to do was face Warrel, but he had to know the truth. If Warrel had survived the Similcue attack, he would be somewhere safe in the palace.

"I'm going with you," said Jenn. "I am the ambassador from Earth."

"Of course you are." Kai hadn't considered going without Jenn.

After their shuttled had touched down on the landing pad of the palace, a security team fanned out ahead of them. Their weapons were out and armed, but it turned out security was not necessary. The building seemed deserted.

Jenn held onto Kai's arm as they walked through the gardens. Even this far inside the interior, they saw no guards and no servants.

"This is strange," said Kai. "I thought we would see someone on patrol." When they arrived at the audience hall, the doors were ajar. They cautiously proceeded down the length of the corridor.

"Is anyone here?" Kai called. His words echoed off the walls, and no one responded to him. "This way." He led the group to a conference room behind the throne. The door was locked.

"Should I blast it open?" asked the security chief.

"I don't think that will be necessary." Kai opened a concealed panel near the door and pressed his palm against it. The door clicked open. "Only a select few have access to this room. I consider myself fortunate that the Emperor thought I was worthy."

Warrel sat at the end of a long conference table. His head rested on the table, and an empty wine bottle lay next to him.

251

Kai strode toward Warrel and checked his pulse.

"Is he dead?"

"Yes. Dead drunk and unconscious." Kai shook Warrel, slowly at first, then more vigorously when he didn't get a response. "Wake up, Warrel! What happened here?

Warrel slowly regained consciousness. When he lifted his head, Jenn saw he hadn't shaved for a few days and his clothes were wrinkled.

"Look who's here," Warrel slurred. "The great Kai Imwaden, Anquera's biggest traitor."

"Where is the council?"

"They decided to save themselves and abandon me. The city is in ruins. The Similcue have destroyed it."

Warrel tried to let his head drop onto the table again, but Kai grabbed his collar and yanked him up.

"You're not done yet. Where did Renquel go?"

"I don't know where anyone went. Away. He left and took his daughter with him. She said she won't marry me now. I'm not enough of a warrior."

"Kai," said Jenn. "Leave him alone. He's not useful like this."

"He wanted to kill you, Jenn."

"At one time, but look at him now. I have my revenge seeing his condition."

He nodded at two of the soldiers. "Take Warrel to his room. It's on the second floor. You can't miss it. It's opulent." They pulled Warrel to his feet. He protested weakly but let them drag him out of the room.

"What are you going to do now?"

"Make some calls and find out why the nobles have turned into cowards."

CHAPTER 33

Kai made call after call on Anquera's communication system trying to contact any of the nobles. No one answered him.

"You're too nice," Jenn said. "You are calling them and leaving messages. Maybe they're avoiding you. You know they see your communications - the system tells you someone's listened to all of them. Kai, these people have responsibilities to the Emperor and their people. It's not right for them to pack up and leave. They need to be here. Start hitting them where it hurts. Tell them to show up tomorrow or you're going to start confiscating their property and money."

"I don't have the authority to do that."

"Do they know that? And besides, if everyone else is gone, and only one person remains, they're effectively the Emperor and the entire government."

"You might be right. What do you know about being too nice, anyway?"

"I used to have that problem myself."

"What happened?"

She smiled. "I met you."

* * * *

Kai recalled the crew from Anquesh ships in orbit to fill positions in the palace until he found regular staff. Soon the building was populated again, with guards in the halls and staff in critical areas. He assigned attendants to Warrel and made sure they kept him out of trouble. Before they went to sleep, they secured the area. Kai called Sevit and asked him to survey the city and surrounding areas.

Before long, Sevit contacted him with a preliminary report. "People have evacuated the city, mostly to the surrounding hills. They have formed tent cities, but they lack food and medical care. Conditions are dreadful."

"Send the doctors down and any extra supplies."

"Already on it, sir. The Earth doctors want to help too."

"Great. Make sure that each one has an Anquesh security guard protecting them, preferably those who can translate. Let's make sure there aren't any accidents."

"Yes, sir."

"I think that is all that can be done for now," said Kai, settling back onto the bed.

"Come here," said Jenn. "You look exhausted."

Kai was about to stretch out and give his recovering body a break when they heard a knock at the door.

"I'm sorry, but you have a call from Minister Renquel."

"Don't take it," said Jenn. "He had his chance earlier. Let him wait."

Kai shook his head. "He has influence, and I need to treat him with the same respect I want to receive." He activated the communications system in his room.

"My security tells me there are Earth ships in orbit around our homeworld."

"Yes, minister. They are our allies now. We helped to defend their planet, and they will assist in the defense of ours. With their help, we have driven off the Similcue. With luck, we took enough of a bite out of them so they won't bother us again."

"I see," said the minister tightly. "Let me ask you a question. Who are you to think you can order me or any of the other nobles around?"

"I'm not asking your permission. Warrel is incoherent. The next in line is the former Emperor's brother, Hanton, but he is missing. Do you know where he is?"

"Hanton was so disgusted with Warrel that he took the rest of the fleet and left."

"You seem to know quite a bit. Are you in communication with Hanton?"

Renquel said nothing.

"Tell Hanton we need him here. If other people are willing to step up, you won't need to listen to my commands."

"You know I can't control what he does."

"It will be better if we work together."

* * * *

By the morning, Warrel had sobered up. Someone had cleaned him and dressed him, and he looked almost respectable again. After inspecting Warrel's appearance, Kai judged he was capable of attending court. One by one, various nobles slowly entered the room. There wasn't a hundred percent attendance, but there were enough to form a quorum.

With Jenn by his side, Kai announced the treaty with Earth was valid and binding. Some of the nobles grumbled, of course.

"Would you rather have the Similcue on your doorstep again? They're gone for now, but we know they're coming back. We need to be ready to fight." Kai pointed his hand at the nobles. "You abandoned your people at the time they needed you the most. Without them, you wouldn't have your positions. To build our government again, we'll have to design a new system, one which includes everyone."

"By whose authority?" protested one of the nobles.

"I have twenty-five warships above this planet giving me the authority. Let's keep things simple. Warrel will remain Emperor, but his powers will. He'll represent Anquera during negotiations with other planets. The nobles have land and wealth, and they'll be allowed to keep it as long as they don't interfere with the new government. We are going to try the Earth system of government and elect legislators from the people. You can either work with us or leave, but change is coming."

No one spoke a word.

"The council is finished." The nobles got to their feet and started milling around the room, grumbling.

"Is this going to work?" Jenn asked.

"It's your idea. Don't you know? I think so. By the time the Similcue return, we'll have pulled together the people and the government will be strong enough to fight them off. Speaking of fights, don't we have an unresolved wedding battle? We need to find out which of us is stronger."

* * * *

It was a typically hot Anquera day when Jenn walked out into the arena for the second and final time in her life. She wasn't nervous now. Jenn looked forward to losing, and becoming Kai's bride. A spectacular future stretched in front of her, offering her opportunities that she would have missed on Earth. She wouldn't only be the Earth's ambassador. The Academy had offered her a position as a physical therapy instructor. During the day, she would help train the first generation of Anquesh therapists. During the night, an alien would ravish her body.

Not bad for an Earth girl.

The people of Anquesh tricked into the stadium, filling the stands. More were watching the broadcast at home. They cheered as she crossed the sand.

Jenn knew the noise was for her. They had watched her fight for Kai's honor the first time. They saw her work to assemble the fragments of the Anquesh Empire into a coherent. And when the people elected Kai Prime Minister, she was by his side again.

In many ways, Jenn had become a symbol of Earth to Anquera. Humans were no longer hated enemies or honored enemies.

They were allies.

Jenn walked to the center of the arena, ready to face her adversary. Kai came out of the tent.

"I love you, sindare. Are you ready?" he asked.

She grinned back at him.

"I love you. I'm always ready for you."

If you enjoyed this book, please review it on Amazon. Your review helps me succeed as an author.

To stay up-to-date on my latest releases, sign up for my newsletter at:

http://lisalace.com/newsletter/

OTHER BOOKS BY LISA LACE

TERRAMATES

Water World Warrior

Taken

Water World Confidential

Alpha's Enslaved Bride

Auctioned to the Alpha

Naima

www.ingramcontent.com/pod-product-compliance
Lightning Source LLC
Chambersburg PA
CBHW020555180626
46810CB00007B/2510